THE WHITE LILY MURDER

When New York department store magnate Cyrus Embrich is found stabbed to death at his office desk, the police have little evidence to go on. Embrich's secretary reveals that her employer had been in fear of his life, and in the event of anything happening to him, he had asked her to call in the famed private investigator 'Probability' Jones to assist the police. Aided — and at times led — by his able assistant Rosanna Beach, Jones finds himself caught up in the most complex and dangerous case of his career . . .

VICTOR ROUSSEAU

THE WHITE LILY MURDER

Complete and Unabridged

LINFORD
Leicester

First published in Great Britain

First Linford Edition
published 2015

A catalogue record for this book is available
from the British Library.

ISBN 978–1–4448–2628–9

Published by
F. A. Thorpe (Publishing)
Anstey, Leicestershire

Set by Words & Graphics Ltd.
Anstey, Leicestershire
Printed and bound in Great Britain by
T. J. International Ltd., Padstow, Cornwall

This book is printed on acid-free paper

1

The Manhattan office occupied by 'Probability' Jones was quite a small one. It consisted of a single, dingy, lighted room on the top story and at the rear of an old-fashioned structure overlooking the elevated. From the window one could glimpse the Bay between two mammoth buildings.

On the glass of the door was: JONES — DETECTIVE.

There were two flat-topped desks, used respectively by Jones and his stenographer. The wall on one side was a mass of many tiers of books, principally dealing with statistics and mathematical treatises.

A little after 9:30 in the morning Jones's stenographer, Miss Rosanna Beach, was looking at her employer's back. Her fingers, which ought to have been playing upon the keys of her machine, were idle. Jones was talking to her with his back turned, and his pen was drawing an extensive series of parallel and crossed lines, which he was filling in abstractedly with what turned out to be a super-series of noughts and crosses.

'I told you on October 14 that, according to computation compiled from available sources, 27 percent of all proposals of marriage lead to marriage, Miss Beach,' said Jones.

Rosanna Beach sighed, and continued to stare fixedly at her employer's broad shoulders, rimmed with a line of white collar and topped by hair of tousled red. Tall, lank, with an auburn shock above a homely face, deeply lined, Jones looked the apotheosis of uninteresting conventionality. He was frequently mistaken for a revivalist, but this was due to a certain intensity of purpose, and a handgrip that could reduce unwary metacarpals to the consistency of paper pulp. His black tailcoat was shiny at the seams, and his whole personality, like his habiliments, appeared in need of pressing.

'I have been figuring that that percentage has now risen to 31 in consequence of the decrease of the male population of this country due to the war,' continued Jones.

Rosanna Beach feigned indignation. 'I suppose you mean that a man's getting to be a prize, because there aren't so many of them,' she said.

'To estimate that,' answered Jones, 'does not fall within the province of the statistician. He deals simply with facts, and leaves the interpretation to others. And yet, this is the most difficult thing to impress upon the mind of the student of the only exact science — that of probability.'

Jones swung round in his chair, and his face became alight with enthusiasm.

'I say 'exact,' because every so-called exact science, other than probability — astronomy and chemistry, for example — shows small, unaccountable divergences from mathematical laws which are the despair of investigations. For example, the atomic weights of the elements, shown by Mendelieff to be an arithmetical progression, do not form an exact arithmetical progression. But when we deal with the laws of probability we enable to make our predictions absolute, granted our data are sufficient. If we coordinate our facts upon a scale sufficiently large, we reduce the variable to the infinitesimally small. You follow me, Miss Beach?'

'I'm trying to,' answered Rosanna truthfully.

'It is by virtue of the exact laws of probability that insurance companies exist. In fact, the whole substructure of our financial world is immediately dependent on these laws. One might say, in fact, that by the laws of probability prophecy is placed among the sciences.'

'Then,' asked Rosanna, with that simple directness which often disconcerts the wise, 'why can't we all make our fortunes at Monte Carlo?'

'Because,' answered Jones earnestly, 'the variables are too numerous, and the opportunities of the casual player too small to permit of a correct estimation. In life insurance we deal with a simple magnitude — the duration of human life. Wars, epidemics may and do affect its mean duration on a limited scale, but the variable magnitude here tends continually to equality with our fixed magnitude by the fact of the immutable laws of life.

'At Monte Carlo, on the other hand, while we have a magnitude of mathematical precision — the ultimate equalization of the two factors of red and black, the variables are innumerable — the lie of the table, the trick of the croupier's hand; and one cannot play continuously for a year, with unlimited capital, in order to eliminate these.

'It is by collating all the variables that one may predict with absolute correctness. For example, within the week ending there will be a murder of a startling character committed somewhere upon Manhattan Island, which may be deferred for ten days by a week of bright sunshine, or a suicide inspired by love, or certain other combinations. The factors may differ, but the product is always constant.'

Rosanna Beach was staring at him with dilated eyes. She looked as if she were going to faint.

'Of course, this may not happen,' Jones continued. 'I do not claim to have weighed every variable in the immense series of social variables that the private detective must consider. My seven years of work has enabled me to cover only a tiny portion of these. But I think you will find that my estimate will prove correct, because the laws of probability are exact.

'Now, to take up the thread of what I was saying, I was commenting upon the fact that the percentage of accepted matrimonial proposals which result in marriage has risen from 27 to 31 in consequence of the war. Nineteen percent of proposals are accepted upon repetition, so far as I can gather from my somewhat obscure sources of information. It is on that I — I —'

Jones' rugged face grew softer. Taking the girl's hand in his, he continued, 'I'm a good mathematician, but a darn poor lover, I know. But this is the second time I've asked you, and there will still be a seven percent chance at the third time of asking, but I — I base my hopes upon the second.'

Rosanna withdrew her hand nervously. 'It — it's impossible, Mr. Jones,' she answered, playing with the ring on her third finger. 'I — I *hoped* you'd understand. I — I've been flashing *this* at you ever since I saw you were — *going* to.'

'Does that mean you're engaged?' asked Jones, with unworldly innocence.

Rosanna nodded. 'And it's just — *infatuation*, Mr. Jones,' she continued. 'Why, you don't know a thing about me; you've only known me six or seven weeks. Why, you took me without references of any kind, because you told me that the variable of forged references was a greater magnitude than the variable of dishonest blonde stenographers! No, I'm not free.'

'That means that you are definitely engaged?'

'I — *I'm not free*,' Rosanna repeated nervously.

'In that case, I shall say no more,' said Jones. 'Twenty-four percent of all engagements are broken off in consequence of a subsequent attraction. But I'm not an attraction and — '

'And you're a gentleman,' said Rosanna, 'and I trust you implicitly. That's why I've been hoping it might still be possible for me to stay with you. I love the work, Mr. Jones, and I'd rather be here than anywhere else, even at a much higher salary.'

'You bet you'll stay!' said Jones. 'You haven't quite mastered the theorem of Laplace which I gave you to study — I could see that — but you're a whale on observation, while I — I — '

'Oh, aren't you a blindy-bat!' said the girl with gentle reproach. 'I always said that, if you're the brains of the combination, I'm the eyes. Remember that Vintner case?'

'I — er — yes, but — '

'I'll never, never forget how you found the very house in which Vintner was hiding, by figuring it out with diagrams, after the police had been baffled for weeks, and then — then you were going to tear up all your records and start a *farm*, because you couldn't see him in the clothes closet.'

Ting-ling!

It was only the telephone, but Rosanna started as if it had been the whine of a shell. Rising from her chair, she went to the instrument and took down the receiver with shaking fingers.

8

Jones leaned back in his chair. '*Damn!*' he muttered inaudibly.

He was 37 years of age, and he had never been in love. His boyhood had been too hard, and his mind, perhaps, too serious. It was only within the three past years that, by the use of his mathematical methods, he had made a name for himself in the solution of mysterious crimes.

Since then fame and patronage had flowed in upon him; even the police occasionally invoked his aid, though they took the credit subsequently. His future seemed secure.

He had loved Rosanna from the moment she applied to him, among thirty-nine other girls, for a position as stenographer. In his mind he knew that he had selected her because of a variable too great for him to master, too potent to be confined in circle or parallelogram — love. He had meant to win her, too.

After she had rejected him the first time, nine days before, he had spent two sleepless nights in a calculation of all possible variables, and he had arrived at the conclusion that he could not fail, by the laws of probability, unless an unknown variable, which he had overlooked, were present.

It was. Jones had overlooked the variable which had the greatest magnitude of all — a prior engagement.

'*Hold the wire!*' Jones heard Rosanna saying. She turned toward him, her voice trembling, her face a mask. 'Cyrus K. Embrich was found murdered in the office of his store this morning,' she said faintly. Then, to Jones's astonishment, she caught at his coat sleeve. 'It's Miss Martin, Mr. Embrich's secretary, speaking. Don't take the case!' she whispered.

'Eh? Why not?' demanded Jones in amazement.

'I'd rather you wouldn't. I know some of those people.'

The telephone, with the receiver hanging, was spluttering like a gagged man trying to scream. Gently detaching himself, Jones stepped to it. 'This is Mr. Jones,' he said.

Reflected in the polished curve of the mouthpiece, Jones saw the tiny figure of Rosanna standing, her hands clasped in front of her, but the distortion of the reflection did not transmit the anguished look in her eyes.

'Yes, Miss Martin,' Rosanna heard him say, 'I certainly . . . but . . . you say he had gone in fear of his life and left positive instructions that I was to be called in if anything happened to him?'

The nasal gurgle of the telephone that followed conveyed no meaning to Rosanna's straining ears.

'I don't believe that I can take the case,' Jones was answering. 'I'm pretty busy, and it's really a police matter — at first, anyway. No, I must positively — '

The whining splutter deepened in tone. A man's voice had replaced Miss Martin's at the other end. Rosanna could make out very little of what was being said, though she had slowly moved forward, as if under compulsion, until she stood beside her employer. Jones's final words, as he hung up the receiver, crushed out all hope in her.

'That was Inspector Clay, of the Homicide Bureau,' he said. 'Headquarters has taken over the case. He wants me in on it at once, and to save trouble all round if I bring you. I don't know why he wants *you*, Miss Beach. Did you tell me you *knew* some of the people concerned?'

Rosanna clasped and unclasped her fingers nervously. 'Yes,' she answered. 'I suppose I'll have to face it. I'll tell you when we get there.'

'All right,' said Jones.

Rosanna put on her hat and rubbers, and they went out of the building. Outside the doors of the downtown department store a huge, jostling throng had already assembled, extending clear across the street, which was lined with stalled cars. A squad of policemen was briskly breaking up the mob.

Within the store the employees stood about in little groups, discussing the murder in low tones. Nearly all the force had come on duty at the time of its discovery, and had been ordered to remain. They were looking toward the staircase which led to the offices on the half-floor which had been built into the rear portion of the ground floor. The air was filled with the subdued hum of voices.

The Embrich department store was an

old-fashioned, five-story structure fronting on Broadway. It had been established about the time when the large department stores were being built, and was thoroughly established. Some ten years before, the premises had been extended by the addition of an annex of the same height, built at the back of the original edifice. The half-floor which contained the offices was situated in this, and the upper stories constituted an extension and enlargement of the original departments. On the ground floor of the annex were the shipping and packing departments, opening into a gated yard, containing the garage for the Embrich fleet of trucks.

Jones and Rosanna went up the staircase. In front of the first door on the left of the passage, which had CYRUS K. EMBRICH and PRIVATE on the glass, two men and a woman were standing. A policeman stood at each of the closed doors.

The woman was about 45 years of age, neatly dressed in a stylish suit. She had a forceful, almost masculine look, and a competent air. The younger man, who

13

appeared to be about 30 years of age, had rather weak features, and thick, loose lips whose ugliness was only accentuated by a small, flaxen mustache, at which he was biting nervously. Jones recognized these two as Ellen Martin, Embrich's secretary and Philip Goodloe, his nephew.

The second man, who wore the uniform of an inspector, was the famous Clay. He was not very tall, but enormously broad, a solidly built figure of about 50, with a broad, flat, pock-marked nose, heavy, jet-black mustache, and dark brown eyes, limpidly and maliciously clear. A look of quiet amusement, the celebrated 'Clay smile' as it had come to be known, was always on his heavy face. Clay looked, out of uniform, like a typical gambler or ward politician, an absurd similarity which was forgotten as soon as one heard his soft, singularly clear bass voice; and Clay had the gift of conveying the impression of possessing a good deal of concealed knowledge.

Clay and Jones exchanged nods. 'Morning, Mr. Jones,' said the inspector. 'Our men have been on the job for nearly an hour past, but the more light we can throw on this business the better. We're waiting for the medical examiner just now.'

He broke off, to look keenly at Rosanna. Goodloe was looking at her with a sort of sheepish scowl.

'Better take a look inside that door, Mr. Jones,' said the inspector. 'Then we'll ask Miss Martin to tell you what she's told me.'

Jones entered the private office. The great bulk of the body that had been Embrich filled the swivel-chair, but was sprawled forward so that the wax-white face was bent over the desk. One hand hung by the side; the other, with crooked fingers, rested upon a pile of papers beside the telephone, as if the murdered man had endeavored, in the last moments of his life, to summon aid, and failed.

Upon the desk in front of the body were two white lilies.

Cyrus K. Embrich appeared to have been killed instantaneously by a thrust between the shoulders into the heart. A little trickle of blood had dripped down the blue serge coat and stained the floor between two small Oriental rugs. The murderer, as if in a panic, seemed to have endeavored to remove the traces of the crime, for the stain upon the boards had been rubbed and scoured, with the only result that it glistened as if it had been veneered.

The implement of murder, a heavy steel envelope-opener with an ivory handle, rested upon the table. There was dried blood upon the handle.

The big safe was open and contained only a few ledgers and bundles of papers. Embrich's gold watch was visible in the gaping waistcoat pocket.

Jones only spent a few moments in the room. He knew that he was incapable of picking up any clues to be discovered by observation. He would need Rosanna's aid for that — and it was evident that the girl was too distraught to aid him at present.

When he went out he saw that she was laboring under an intense strain. She was almost as white as the dead man in the room. She was standing with one hand against the wall of the passage, for support, and her eyes shifted quickly from one face to another.

Philip Goodloe's eyes were cast down, Ellen Martin was staring ahead of her, and Inspector Clay watched the trio with his sardonic smile.

'Well — you saw, Mr. Jones? A bad business!' said the inspector. He turned to the secretary. 'Miss Martin, since Mr. Jones is in this, tell him as much as you've told me,' he said.

'I'll try,' said the secretary in a strained voice. 'Mr. Embrich and I had been associated for about fifteen years, and I knew everything about the business. In fact, I can say without hesitation that he placed absolute confidence in me.

'I have a key to his private office. Our two offices, you will see, Mr. Jones, are intercommunicating, and cut off from the others. Mr. Embrich couldn't bear to have bustle and confusion about him. Anyone who wanted to see him, even the principal buyers or the departmental managers, had to come through my room. His door was always locked. When he went in or out, he locked it immediately. Generally nobody knew whether he was in his office or not, unless they watched for him.

'You observed the partitions, Mr. Jones? They look like thin wood, but they're nearly soundproof. That was a fad of Mr. Embrich's. The only thing that didn't disturb him was the sounds from the yard. It was people moving along the corridors that got on his nerves.

'He had been working a good deal at night of late. When I went home yesterday evening he told me that he expected to remain here until about 10 o'clock. Nobody could follow the market as he could. He seemed quite cheerful.

'That was the last I saw of him alive. It was about half-past six, and I had brought him a cup of tea and some sandwiches on a tray from the restaurant on the top floor. I always did that when he stayed late; he never permitted anyone else to bring him his supper.'

'Why not?' asked Jones.

'He didn't like Lumpkin, the restaurant manager, because he had once served him some fried potatoes dripping with grease.

Mr. Embrich had many little fads, and he took quick likes and dislikes, but he was a just man and very considerate to everybody.'

'Who took the tray away?' queried the inspector.

'Lumpkin removed it from my room this morning. Mr. Embrich always put the tray in my room when he had finished with it, and locked the communicating door again. My outer door is always open. So Lumpkin, of course, had no idea that poor Mr. Embrich was lying dead in there.'

'I see,' said Clay. 'But why does your restaurant manager have to carry his own trays about the building?'

'Because our restaurant is only a small affair, for the employees, not the purchasers. There are only Lumpkin and two or three waiters, but the waiters were gone for the day. It's really just a lunch counter, where food is served at cost price.'

'Now, why did Mr. Embrich always carry the tray into your room when he had finished with it?' asked Jones.

'It was just part of his orderly ways. He couldn't have worked with a used tray in his office. He'd have had a fit if he'd come in and found it there in the morning.'

'Go on, Miss Martin,' said the inspector.

'This morning I arrived at the office about five minutes to nine. My times vary only by a minute or so. I've learned to be as methodical as Mr. Embrich. I went in by the door leading to my room, of course. There was a telephone message on my desk — '

'You said your door was always open?' Jones interposed.

'Yes. All private papers were kept in Mr. Embrich's room, and important ones in the safe, to which we two alone had the combination. The door between our offices is always locked. The telephone message was from our Philadelphia representative, asking for information about a line of satins. Jenny Friend, who works in Mr. Timson's department, and answers calls in my room before the operator arrives, had written out the message and left it for me a few minutes before. The switchboard is put out of connection every night, and all calls come straight through to my office. I unlocked the door between Mr. Embrich's office and mine, to get the information, and saw at once what — had happened.'

'Go on, Miss Martin. Take your own time,' said Clay.

'I saw that Mr. Embrich was dead,' continued Miss Martin in a low tone. 'I went out, stunned, and sat down in my room to think. I have been trained to keep my self-control, and not act precipitately. I went back and opened the safe. I saw that it had not been tampered with. There was nothing of any value in it, except some receipts and commercial papers, and I took some of them out and put them in my office. I left the safe door open. I locked the connecting door and left the store, and telephoned the police from the drugstore on the next block. I thought it best to give out no information here.'

'Very well,' said Clay. 'And the two lilies were lying on the desk?'

'Yes. What do they mean? Who can

have put them there, and why?'

Clay smiled, as if he suspected more than he was prepared to tell. 'I guess they're just a blind,' he answered. 'That covers about what you've told me already, Miss Martin. Now suppose we all take another look inside.'

'And Miss Beach?' Jones inquired, seeing that Rosanna was on the verge of a breakdown.

Rosanna solved that problem for herself. As Clay swung open the door of Embrich's office, disclosing the form in the chair, Rosanna, with a wild outburst of grief, ran into the room and flung herself upon her knees beside the body, sobbing, and clasping the icy hand in hers.

2

With an expressive shrug of his shoulders, Inspector Clay motioned to the others to precede him, and closed the door behind him. Rosanna, weeping hysterically, kneeled beside the chair. She rose to her feet, pulling herself together with a visible effort.

'I — I want to explain my own connection with — with this,' she began. 'I feel so wretched and wicked. I never dreamed, when I ran away from Uncle Cy, that I should return to find him like — like *this*. When I went to your office, Mr. Jones, in answer to your advertisement, I didn't tell you that my father was Edmund Beach, Mr. Embrich's former partner. After my father's death, Mr. Embrich adopted me under an old arrangement embodied in the terms of my father's will. In fact, I had lived with Mr. Embrich for nearly seven years, until recently. Mr. Embrich was very fond of me, but he was self-willed and arbitrary. I

— I'm doing right in telling about this, Philip?' she continued, glancing at the younger man with a humility that made Jones, who caught the look, irrationally angry.

A scowl of annoyance passed over Philip Goodloe's features. 'I guess it'll *all* have to come out — what isn't known already. And that's precious little,' he answered.

'And, of course, the more light we have, the better for all parties concerned,' said Inspector Clay suavely.

'Well, Mr. Embrich always had it in his mind that Philip and I were to marry,' Rosanna continued. 'But after we became engaged, a little trouble developed — '

'Which is at present under lock and key,' said Clay sardonically, jerking his thumb toward the other side of the corridor.

'I had studied stenography because I had foreseen that I might not always wish to be dependent upon Mr. Embrich. So I left home secretly and took a position with Mr. Jones.'

'And you were all wrong, Anna,'

Goodloe muttered. 'I never cared a thing about the girl. There was nothing to it at all — not in the way you thought . . . '

He broke off. Rosanna ceased speaking also, and, as if incapable of more, fixed her eyes intently on the inspector's face.

'You know something about this little trouble, no doubt, Miss Martin?' asked Clay.

'I can't speak with authority, of course,' the secretary answered. 'But naturally, I've been in a position to see a good deal. I understand that Miss Beach was annoyed over Mr. Goodloe's attentions to the Miss Friend whom I've referred to — '

'I'm sure *I don't care!*' Rosanna cried. 'It was only that — that Mr. Embrich insisted *we* were to marry, and — '

'But you are engaged to Mr. Goodloe? Isn't that the ring he gave you?' inquired Clay, casting his sardonic look at the girl's finger.

'I did accept this at Philip's request to please Uncle Cy, but it was distinctly understood between us that — that it was not to signify that we were — were actually — '

'Still wearin' it, I notice, though! Nice little ring!' said Clay pleasantly.

Rosanna flushed, but said nothing. Goodloe's scowl deepened. Jones was conscious of a medley of emotions.

'Will you proceed, Miss Martin?' asked Clay quietly.

'Miss Beach left her home without warning. She notified Mr. Embrich of the possibility of her taking some such step, I understand, but he treated it as a joke. He was very much attached to her. Of course he couldn't advertise the fact that she had gone, and he was worried over his inability to trace her. I did suggest our calling in Mr. Jones, of course, not knowing that Miss Beach was actually employed by him, but Mr. Embrich said he wouldn't put detectives on the trail of a woman. He had had enough of that.'

'How's that?'

'He spoke of his half-brother's divorce.' She glanced with hesitation at Philip Goodloe.

'Oh, don't mind *me*! Trot out the family skeleton!' said Goodloe savagely.

'Perhaps you'd better tell us, Miss

Martin,' said the inspector. 'Of course it's confidential, and anything that lets in a ray of light is best for all.'

'*I'll tell you!*' said Goodloe viciously. 'My *father* was Mr. Embrich's half-brother. He married my mother out West. She went wrong, and he put detectives on her trail and caught her. She ran away, and he got a divorce. Afterward he shot himself, and Mr. Embrich adopted me. There it is in a nutshell!'

He glared about him as he spoke. The callous reference to his mother, and his willingness to tell the story, filled Jones with disgust. He had taken an intense dislike to the young man, a dislike which had no mathematical basis whatever.

'Now, you *fool*, go on and blurt out something *else*!' said Goodloe to the secretary.

The hurt look in Miss Martin's eyes was extraordinary for one of her masculine appearance and temperament. 'I'm sorry, Philip — ' she began.

'And none of you saw or heard anything more about Miss Beach until this morning?' asked the inspector.

'Mr. Embrich never met her again. I believe she sent him a note, telling him that she was happy and earning her own living — '

Rosanna nodded mutely. Her eyes were full of tears, and there was intense misery in them as she turned them slowly toward the form in the chair.

'There wasn't any other reason for your leaving home, I suppose, except that little trouble with Mr. Goodloe?' Clay asked.

Whether this was a shaft at a venture or not, the question seemed paralyzing. Rosanna's lip trembled. She made no attempt to answer. After a moment Miss Martin intervened.

'Perhaps I could answer that question better than Miss Beach,' she said.

She hesitated, and continued: 'Mr. Embrich was a bachelor, and he'd been rather gay in his younger days. He always had an appreciative eye for a good-looking girl. I think Miss Beach felt just a little resentment about Miss Friend, who sometimes acted as Mr. Embrich's stenographer, because I had much of the management on my hands. Once or twice, when he was confined to his house, he sent for her to take dictation there.

'I know there was nothing more to it than that, but Miss Beach didn't like it. I was always in and out of the house, and I saw a good deal of what was going on. Miss Friend is very pretty. Mr. Embrich was a very kind man, especially to his employees, and very good to his girls. There were others he took an interest in. But his past reputation was against him, and he didn't realize that he was sometimes compromising them, and causing talk.'

'Quite so!' said Clay. 'That's where you met Miss Friend?' he asked Philip Goodloe.

'I saw her at the house once or twice.'

'Took her to supper?'

'I took her out once, more in fun than anything else,' growled Goodloe.

'Auto riding?'

'See here, what's that got to do with this — ?'

'How many times?' pursued Inspector Clay remorselessly.

'I can't remember. Twice, perhaps — maybe three times. She was just a good-looking girl I'd met, and I was depressed over Rosanna's attitude.'

'Quite so!' said Clay again. There was a wealth of quiet malice in his tone. 'Now, Miss Martin, there's one point we haven't touched on since Mr. Jones came in. You were saying over the phone that Mr. Embrich had gone in fear of his life, and wanted him called in if anything happened. How about that?'

'Mr. Embrich was grateful to Mr. Jones for having saved him a lot of money about eight months ago, when he was being robbed. A man named Vintner was run down through Mr. Jones's methods. Vintner was one of our employees. Mr. Embrich was highly pleased with Mr. Jones's work. As a result, Vintner was sent up for six months. He had threatened Mr. Embrich subsequently to his release. Yesterday afternoon I saw him in the yard from my window. I went down and warned Mr. Clark, of the shipping department, to tell Mann, the watchman, when he came on duty that evening. Vintner was trying to get his job back — just trading on Mr. Embrich's generosity. And then, I was afraid Vintner had heard some stories about Mr. Embrich and Miss Friend — and would have another reason for vindictiveness. He and the girl had been going together.'

'You think there was something to Mr. Embrich's fears for his life, then? I mean, in connection with his murder?'

'I'm sure of it!' said the secretary emphatically.

'Mr. Embrich had a quarrel with Mr. Goodloe yesterday afternoon, I understand. Please give us your version of it.'

'*Say!*' interposed Goodloe. 'I guess I can tell my own story.'

'You'll have plenty of opportunity, I'm sure, Mr. Goodloe,' returned Clay suavely. 'Just at present I should prefer to have this information from an unbiased witness. You'll understand, I'm sure — '

The ringing of the telephone interrupted the conversation. The inspector picked up the receiver and listened for a moment. 'Send it over right away!' he barked. He hung the receiver up and turned to Miss Martin again. 'Now, about that quarrel!' he demanded.

31

Miss Martin hesitated. 'Of course, I couldn't help hearing what was said,' she began.

'Naturally not,' returned the inspector smoothly. 'It was a violent altercation, I understand?'

'You couldn't call it that. Mr. Goodloe was quite cool. Mr. Embrich was angry, but hardly what might be described as violent. He accused Mr. Goodloe of being the cause of Miss Beach's disappearance, through his running after Jenny Friend.'

'That's the damn lie I'm trying to nail!' shouted Goodloe heatedly.

'Yes, Miss Martin. And Mr. Goodloe reproached his uncle for the same thing?'

'He — he let fall something about that,' faltered the secretary.

'Mr. Embrich then threatened to cut Mr. Goodloe out of his will?'

'Well, he said something about a legacy. I couldn't hear it all. And I didn't make a point of listening. But I know he wanted Miss Beach found. You see, once an idea got into Mr. Embrich's head, he was quite unreasonable about it. He wanted to perpetuate the partnership that he had founded with Mr. Beach.'

'Thank you,' said Clay. 'I guess that'll be all for the present. I'll just ask you to wait in your office until the medical examiner comes.'

'See here,' cried Goodloe, 'I've had just about enough of this! I'm not going to follow you around like a dog while you're snuffling on the trail! I demand that you either place me under arrest or let me go home!'

Clay surveyed him with his leisurely glance. 'What makes you think you're under suspicion, Mr. Goodloe?' he asked.

'I'm not a fool! I told you when I let you take my fingerprints this morning that I'd probably picked up that letter-opener while I was talking to Mr. Embrich yesterday!' Goodloe shouted.

There was a brisk tap at the door. A messenger from headquarters came in with an envelope, which he handed to the inspector, who tore it open, glanced at the contents, nodded, and put it in his pocket. As the messenger withdrew Clay turned back to Goodloe.

'Very well, Mr. Goodloe. I'll take you in

for the present,' he answered suavely. 'Larrigan!'

★ ★ ★

Goodloe had departed in charge of the policeman whom Clay summoned before the others had recovered from their surprise. Rosanna and Miss Martin broke the silence together. The secretary uttered a sort of straining cry, and clinched her fingertips on Clay's sleeve.

'It wasn't him! I'll swear he didn't do it!' she cried. 'Can't you see it was Vintner? I thought it was perfectly plain! Who else had the motive? Who else hated poor Mr. Embrich?'

'It couldn't have been Philip!' exclaimed Rosanna doggedly. 'I've known him since he was a boy. Philip isn't a murderer!'

Clay looked momentarily embarrassed at this outbreak. 'I'm not saying he did it,' he conceded. 'But this report says it's his fingerprints found on that opener. Maybe it's as he says — he left his traces when he was talking with Mr. Embrich. Anyway, we can't take chances.' He turned to Jones.

'I guess we'll see Mr. Timson before going the round, if you're agreeable,' he said. 'He seems sort of peeved at being held.'

'By all means,' murmured Jones.

Clay stepped to the door, opened it, and spoke to one of the policemen. A few moments later Mr. Timson entered. He was a tall, bald, middle-aged man with a hanging mustache and a slight stoop. His air was at once bristling and dejected.

'I'd like to know by what authority I've been arrested and cooped up in — ' he began aggressively. Then, at the sight of the body in the chair, he leaped violently back, and his face assumed an aspect of almost comical terror.

'Mr. Timson,' answered Clay blandly, 'I have a few questions for you.'

Timson tried to compose himself, turning his body resolutely away from the sight of the dead man.

'You are, I believe, assistant manager of this store, under Miss Martin?'

'That's right, Inspector, but I — '

'How long have you been employed here?' Clay's voice was as smooth as honey.

'Twenty-seven years — almost from the beginning. I started in as a boy and grew up with the firm.'

'Mr. Embrich had unlimited confidence in you?'

'He certainly did. You see, I — '

'And how long has Jenny Friend been employed by you?' continued Clay, whose smile was growing blander as Mr. Timson's nervousness increased.

'I'd have to look up her record, but I should guess two or three months, certainly no longer. She came — '

'Ever see *that* before?' asked Clay softly, pointing to the cutter.

'Why, certainly!' stammered Timson. 'It's my own envelope-opener. Mr. Embrich gave it to me when he came back from Europe, and I use it for the heavy mail packages we get.'

'When did you miss it?'

'I haven't missed it.'

'You had it last night?'

'I think so.'

'You *think* so!' repeated Clay sardonically.

Timson flushed and shifted under the

inspector's scrutiny. 'I'm sure — yes, I know I had it when the late mail came in,' he answered.

'Have you any idea how it got here?'

'No, I can only suppose that somebody brought it here,' snapped Timson.

'That sounds reasonable,' said Clay mildly. 'When did you last see Mr. Embrich?'

'About half past five yesterday. I wanted to talk to him — I mean, I didn't see him at all yesterday,' Timson corrected, 'except for a minute or so in the morning. I heard his voice when I was in Miss Martin's office. She said he couldn't see anybody else that day.'

'Why do you suppose that was?'

'Well, I understood that he was upset over some trouble he had been having with Mr. Goodloe,' said the assistant manager reluctantly.

'You heard them?'

'*Everybody* did. They were yelling at the top of their voices.'

'What time was this?'

'I should say between half past four and five.'

'Seemed angry, eh?'

'Well, Mr. Embrich seemed angrier than Mr. Goodloe.'

'You heard the gist of their conversation?'

'I heard them shouting at each other. They were quarreling about some woman. I couldn't distinguish much of what was being said. Mr. Embrich's office is supposed to be sound-proof, and it deadened their voices.'

'You heard no names mentioned?'

Timson hesitated. 'I didn't, but somebody told me afterward that Miss Friend's name had been mentioned by Mr. Embrich. I understand Mr. Goodloe is acquainted with her.'

'Thank you, Mr. Timson. You may go home now. Sorry to have *inconvenienced* you,' he added maliciously.

Timson turned pasty white as he made his way to the door. 'See that Mr. Timson is allowed to go home, O'Reilly!' Clay called over the assistant manager's shoulder. 'Now, if you're willing, we'll look around the shop,' he said. 'I'm sure the ladies needn't — '

'I should prefer to go with you,' said Miss Martin, with an effort.

'Just as you please. Very glad to have you,' answered Clay. He glanced at Rosanna. Until the moment before she had been standing still, as if overcome with horror; but now, mastering herself, she was bending deliberately over the dead man and examining the wound. She crossed the room and looked at the walls, stooped, and inspected the floor beside the swivel-chair, as if hardly aware of the presence of anyone else.

Clay, who rarely registered surprise, glanced at Jones with raised eyebrows.

'Miss Beach is a very valuable aid to me,' Jones explained. 'It was really she who found Vintner in that little affair before.'

Clay pursed his lips and nodded. 'I guess we'll go and have a chat with this man Lumpkin,' said the inspector pleasantly.

They left the office, Miss Martin leading the way, and passed along the gallery toward the elevators. Underneath, a sea of faces was upturned toward them.

Confused whispers arose. The elevators were not running, and they ascended the stairs to the top floor, passing an officer on guard, and approaching the restaurant through the toy department.

The restaurant proved to be nothing more than a lunch counter, with a few oilcloth-covered tables. Lolling against the counter was Lumpkin, the manager, in nervous conversation with the morning waiter. The manager started nervously at the sight of Clay in uniform.

Clay dismissed the waiter with a wave of the hand, comprehensive enough to send him scuttling into invisibility. 'Well, Mr. Lumpkin,' he boomed, laying his hand on the manager's shoulder, 'what can you tell us about this? *You* didn't kill Mr. Embrich?' he inquired genially.

Lumpkin, a nervous, consumptive-looking Pole with a pasty forehead edged by receding hair, trembled. 'I swear I don't know nothing, Inspector!' he answered.

'Of course you don't! Your job lies here, don't it? Did you provide supper for Mr. Embrich last night?'

Lumpkin glanced fearfully at the

40

secretary. 'Miss Martin, she tell me to cut some sandwiches — ' he began.

'What time was this?'

'Soon after six. I was just closing up, and she tell me to cut some sandwiches and make a cup of tea for Mr. Embrich. He always wanted the same, and I mustn't put no fat in, or there'd be hell to pay. Miss Martin, she took down the tray. Then I went home. I was sick last night with a cold. My wife will tell you. I stayed in bed — '

'You got the tray this morning?'

'Yes, sir, out of Miss Martin's room. Mr. Embrich always put it there when he was through.'

'Was the door between Miss Martin's office and Mr. Embrich's office locked?'

Lumpkin swallowed. 'Sure!' he answered.

Clay, whose hand had never left the manager's shoulder, swung him gently toward the window and looked into his eyes. 'How do you know, Lumpkin?' he asked in his soft voice. 'What did you try the door for?'

'I didn't try; is always locked,' stammered the Pole.

Clay grunted. 'And what's this I hear about Mr. Embrich not liking your fried potatoes?' he demanded.

3

Lumpkin started violently. Beads of sweat glistened upon his forehead. 'That was a long time ago — two, three months,' he faltered. 'Mr. Embrich said they was greasy, even though I'd drained every drop of fat off them. Mr. Embrich snapped at me, and since then he wouldn't let me bring in his tray no how.'

'And you were afraid of losing your job, eh?'

Lumpkin was trembling. 'I swear I didn't kill him!'

'I believe you, Lumpkin. So you're sure you know nothing about it, eh?'

'Oh, my God!' groaned the restaurant manager. 'I stay on the top floor and don't interfere with what's going on downstairs. When my work's through I go home to my wife and stay in bed all the evening to make me strong. You ask her!'

'Guess we'll take your word for that part, Lumpkin,' said the inspector genially.

'So you don't suspect anybody?'

'I dunno who'd want to kill Mr. Embrich. I minds my own business up here, and I gots all the job I can do, with them girls and fellers complainin' about the coffee and sandwiches.' His shifty black eyes, glancing out beneath his pasty forehead beaded with sweat, looked like a trapped rat's.

'Cold better now?' asked Clay.

Lumpkin gulped an affirmation.

'Then you'd better go home to bed to stop it getting bad again,' said Clay. 'Go get your coat on. And tell your waiter — *Come here!*' he shouted to the shadowy figure that vanished between a giant Noah's Ark and a rocking horse.

The waiter shambled forward. 'You two men can go home,' said the inspector. 'Go straight out of the store, and don't stop to gossip with anybody. Get me?'

It was evident that Lumpkin did. Released from his ordeal, he scurried like a frightened rabbit. Clay spoke a few words to the policeman on duty, instructing him to have the two passed outside. Then the party went down the stairs again to the gallery, and turned back into the corridor.

'Now I guess we'll take a look at the backyard and the Fothergill Street entrance,' said Clay to Jones.

They passed along the corridor, with its closed doors guarded by policemen. From behind them came the murmur of voices. A few of the clerical force had arrived at the time the murder was discovered, principally the girls of the general room, where addressing and folding was done, and these had been included in Clay's general detention orders. At the end of the passage a swinging door opened on a flight of stone steps which led down to the yard.

They stopped before the door. Rosanna immediately began making the same close scrutiny that she had made in Embrich's office, bending over the floor, on which, leading toward the stone stairs, and growing fainter as they approached them, were the tracks of muddy boots.

'Whoever did the job brought in a good deal of mud with them,' said Clay. 'There was an overflow from a choked pipe up the street yesterday afternoon. Brought in too much *wet mud*, I might say — it doesn't show the outlines of the feet plain enough.'

While Rosanna continued her examination, Clay turned his sardonic gaze on Jones. 'I guess all this isn't in *your* line, Mr. Jones,' he said. 'Of course, all *you* have to do is to sit back in your chair and figure it all out with *diagrams*, but I'm trying to put you wise from the *practical* point of view. Ya see, all that mud got scraped off in the passage; there's no marks of it near the stairs, or leading up to the offices. If it'd been a little drier, we could have told the size and shape of the boots of the man that made it.'

'There's something beside the boot tracks,' said Jones. 'Looks as if he brought a dog in with him.'

Clay sniffed. 'Brought a woman,' he answered. 'Those are from a woman's rubbers. Unusual pattern, but not enough to identify the wearer beyond suspicion. Most rubbers have crisscrossed soles. Those are circles. Take a look!'

Clay, seeing that Rosanna was apparently satisfied, turned and led the party down two or three steps into the yard.

In this was the garage, with the trucks in hangars, and a small shanty of a sentry box, used by the watchman when he was not making his rounds. A wooden platform outside the packing-rooms, from which the trucks were loaded, was heaped high with bundles. A number of employees in shirt-sleeves could be seen at work through the dirty windows. Clark, the manager, was seated at a high desk on a stool. It was evident that the fact of Mr. Embrich's death had not paralyzed the activities of his department.

Between the stairs which the party had descended and the entrance to the packing and shipping department ran a narrow passage communicating with the yard at one end, and Fothergill Street on the other. There were no doors between it and the yard, but at the other end an officer stood on guard near a substantial one, which was fastened by bolts at top and bottom, and had also a chain, and a lock with an enormous key. Along the wall, upon a rather low shelf, were ranged six fire-buckets, three parts full of dirty water.

They went down into the yard. A pair of gates, now closed, were topped with iron spikes, and appeared insurmountable except by means of a ladder. High walls extending from them ran along the south side of the premises. The north and east sides of the yard were bounded by the massive Embrich Building itself.

'That'll be the window of Mr. Embrich's office, Miss Martin?' asked Clay, pointing upward.

'That is Mr. Embrich's window, and the next one is mine,' answered the secretary. 'The next three belong to the general offices.'

'Not much chance of anyone getting in that way,' commented Clay. 'Nor over those gates, unless the patrolman and watchman were both asleep.'

The straight brick wall was quite unclimbable. It ran up for twenty-five feet to the windows without affording the smallest foothold.

Rosanna had slipped into the watchman's shanty. The interior was bare, except for a wooden bench. She came back to Miss Martin.

'What sort of character is Mann — sporting?' she asked.

'Just the reverse,' answered Miss Martin. 'He conducts revival meetings over in Flatbush, I believe.'

Clay, who had been listening, grinned. 'Nothing doing in the sports line for Mann!' he said. 'I happen to know him. He's a hellfire street preacher.'

They turned back into the building. Clay led the way, Rosanna following closely behind, and a little in advance of the others. As they passed the shelf on which the fire-buckets were standing, the inspector, by a maladroit swing of his arms, succeeded in tipping one of them over. He shouted, grasped the girl by the arm and dragged her back, just in time to save her from the deluge of dirty water, which nevertheless splashed her skirt.

'I beg *pardon*, Miss Beach!' exploded Clay. 'I'm gettin' a clumsy fool in my old age. It's fortunate I managed to save you, or you'd have been drenched through. Lemme see! Well, I guess that'll dry out all right.'

'It doesn't matter,' said Rosanna,

looking at him in some bewilderment.

Clay stepped to the door of the packing-rooms. The clerks were gazing curiously at the party. 'I've knocked down one of your buckets, Mr. Clark,' he called. 'Perhaps one of your boys would clean up the mess. I'd do it myself if I hadn't my tunic on.'

'No problem, Inspector,' called Clark, stepping toward the door. He was a brisk, well setup man of about 40, spruce and quick in his movements. 'One of you boys get some rags, quick, and clean that mess up. You ready to see me now?'

'In a minute,' Clay answered. 'You know Mr. Jones? He's on this case with me. Give him any information he asks for. I've just one or two questions to ask you myself. Of course you didn't know anything about this till you got here this morning?'

'Not a thing,' said Clark.

'Where do you live?'

'Plainfield.'

'What time did you leave last night?'

'On the 8:48.'

'Usual hour?'

'I've been leaving all sorts of hours the last week or two, on account of the spring rush. Generally I get away before 6:30. Sometimes I stay till nine o'clock.'

'I guess we'll accept that, Mr. Clark,' said Clay, smiling. 'What do you know about this man Vintner?'

'Vintner had a job with us for about nine months,' answered the manager. 'Quiet, steady sort of fellow. Used to drive one of the vans. There was some serious thieving going on, which seemed to be the work of a gang. It was a long time before Vintner was suspected.

'We traced some of the stolen goods to him through the fence who was receiving them. Weren't you on the case, Mr. Jones? Seems I remember you.'

'That's correct,' answered Jones, who had the congenital defect, impossible in any other sort of detective, of hardly ever remembering a face.

Clay interposed. 'Vintner was sent up for six months. When did he come out?'

'About three weeks ago.'

'He's been here since?'

'He has. He came here almost as soon

51

as he was set at liberty, asking for his job back. He hinted he'd been used as a tool, and said it was up to Mr. Embrich to live up to his principles. There's a nerve for you! What staggered me was that he seemed sure he'd get it.'

'How do you mean, exactly?' asked Clay.

Clark hesitated for the first time. 'Well, I dunno,' he answered, 'but he gave the impression of having some sort of pull with somebody inside, that gave him a sort of power. Maybe it was all bluff, though. Anyway, when I turned him down he lay in wait for Mr. Embrich.'

'He came to Mr. Embrich's house on one occasion,' Miss Martin interposed. 'Fortunately I happened to be there; I sent him about his business pretty quickly.'

'The trouble was,' said Clark, 'Mr. Embrich was too easy. Anybody with a sad story could make him put his hand in his pocket.'

'He didn't succeed in seeing Mr. Embrich, as far as you know?' asked Clay.

'I guess not. He got no encouragement

here. He started up the stairs once, and I brought him down by the collar. I don't like to be hard on a man who's down and out, but I told him not to come around here again.'

'You saw him yesterday afternoon?'

'Well, I didn't, but Miss Martin saw him in the yard from her window and came to warn me. She asked me to tell Mann. She said if he came again she'd take the responsibility of having him arrested. I told Mann when I went off duty.'

'Afraid he intended some harm?' Clay asked.

'Yes. He'd threatened to get even. He seemed somehow to feel he hadn't been treated right in being sent up the river, though Mr. Embrich had gone to court and asked for a light sentence. Had something against him on account of one of the young ladies, too. Nonsense, of course. Mr. Embrich wasn't that sort of man.'

'None of your boys saw Vintner yesterday?'

'No. I asked them. But, with the yard

full of trucks, and men coming and going all the time, there's nothing strange in that.'

'How long ago was it that he last threatened Mr. Embrich?'

'About a week, I'd say. I told him not to come back. That was the time I brought him downstairs by the collar.'

'Now, another point: Did you see Mr. Goodloe here yesterday?'

'I did. He came in about 4:30, and went up the stairs to the offices. I don't know what time he came down. We were pretty busy with our deliveries.'

'After Mr. Goodloe went upstairs, did you hear anything like a quarrel?'

'I didn't, but some of the girls were talking about it when they came down. They said it could be heard all through the offices. Mr. Embrich shouting and pounding his fist. He was very excitable.'

'Did they say that Mr. Goodloe threatened Mr. Embrich?'

Clark shook his head. 'I didn't hear that,' he declared.

'All right. We won't keep you any longer. See that you and the boys go out by the yard.' He turned to Jones. 'Maybe you'd like to ask Mr. Clark something?' he suggested.

Jones shook his head. 'I guess you know how to handle them,' he answered.

'Thanks,' said the inspector briefly. 'Now, if you're all satisfied — ' He glanced into the yard. An old man, accompanied by an officer, was just coming in at the gate. 'We've still got two witnesses to see,' he continued, 'and here comes the first of 'em. I guess we'll see Mann upstairs. We can get at things better in that office.'

The party had just returned to the office, with its hideous evidence of death, when the officer announced Mann.

'Bring him in,' said Clay.

He glanced keenly at the rather sleepy-looking watchman who entered. Mann was about 60, of the faithful bulldog type; short, sturdy, with striking dark eyes and clear complexion, and an undercurrent of fire beneath his stolid exterior.

'Sit down, Mann. Sorry to drag you out of bed as soon as you'd turned in,' said Clay.

Mann, catching sight of Embrich's

body, started, recoiled, and gasped. He fixed his eyes on it in horror, and then, approaching softly, as if fascinated, stared at the wound.

'By the Big Man, *he's dead!*' he cried. 'And they neffer told me why they wanted me. Nine years I've worked for him, and a better master no man neffer had! Neffer a Christmas, Mr. Embrich, sir, but a fine goose or turkey, and neffer a month but 'twas, 'Come up to the house, or send your woman, Mann, I've some clothes I won't be needing,' or, 'Send that kid of yours down to the store this afternoon, Mann. He'll want a smart suit to go to the school.' And now you're dead!' He faced Clay with streaming cheeks. 'He wass a goot man, sir,' he said with simple pathos.

'I've one or two questions to ask you. What time did you come on duty last night?'

'At eight o'clock.'

'Did Mr. Clark say anything to you?'

'He did. Told me that Vintner had been hanging about the shop, asking for a job, and threatening Mr. Embrich.'

'Why?'

'He'd been sent up for six months for robbing Mr. Embrich last year, sir.'

'Did you hear that Vintner had any other reason for hating Mr. Embrich?'

'No.'

'You remain on the premises all night?'

'I do. I go through the premises every hour or so.'

'There is a side entrance on Fothergill Street, leading into the passage behind the shipping department. At what time do you lock that?'

'Generally about half past eight, sir, when they're working late in the shipping department. But Mr. Embrich has been going out that way about ten o'clock, when he's stays late, and I have to lock up after him. I have to watch for him, because he doesn't call me when he goes out.'

'What time did you lock the Fothergill Street door last night, Mann?' Clay inquired.

'It was a quarter to ten, or maybe ten. I found the door unfastened, and I supposed Mr. Embrich had gone home.'

'At what time had you previously locked it?'

Mann hesitated. 'I can't lie,' he said. 'I

hadn't locked it before, because I thought Mr. Clark was staying late. But I guess he only turned back to warn me about Vintner.'

'Then the door remained unlocked until nearly ten? Do you know it was found unlocked this morning?'

Mann started. 'No, I — I — '

'I guess you thought it was all right and didn't examine it again. You heard no sound from Mr. Embrich's office — no cry?'

'Not a sound.'

'You did your duty, Mann, and you've told me all I want to know. Go back home,' said Clay.

Mann burst out: 'Go home to sleep, with *him* sitting there with a big hole in his back? Neffer a wink I'll sleep till you've got the scum that did it.'

Miss Martin, as if overcome by what she had gone through, suddenly slipped down in a chair. Her face went white. Rosanna bent over her and took her by the arm. Weeping hysterically, the secretary suffered herself to be led into her own room.

Jones, at Clay's signal, followed him out of the office and, passing into the passage, turned toward a door on the right, which was guarded by a policeman. It was the office of the sub-manager, Timson, consisting of a large room with two windows facing Fothergill Street, and several desks. A door, partly open, gave access to a smaller room, with Timson's name printed on the ground glass.

Beside the nearer of the windows sat a slim, blonde girl. She sat perfectly still, staring out of the window. Her face was averted, but the profile looked uncommonly attractive, and great coils of fair hair were pressed tightly above her ears. In the room with her sat one of the detectives from headquarters: a short, dark, keen-looking man.

'Been talking, Myers?' asked Clay.

'Not a word, sir.'

Inspector Clay went quietly up to the girl and stopped within a foot or two of her, remaining there perfectly motionless for several seconds.

'Jenny!' he said softly.

She shuddered and, as if compelled by

Clay's personality, turned her head slowly and met his eyes for a moment. Her own eyes were blue, limpid and very large. She had a face of extraordinary prettiness. Her eyes were full of tears, but her expression was hard and defiant — frightened, too.

Clay nodded in his grim fashion, a quiet smile upon his saturnine face. 'Well, Jenny, been thinkin' it over?' he asked. 'There's no sense goin' on this way.'

'I've nothing to say!' cried the girl fiercely. 'You and your men can question me till doomsday, and I'll have the same answer for you,' answered the girl wearily. 'I didn't know that Mr. Embrich — ' She caught her breath. 'I tell you I didn't know anything that happened till I got here this morning.'

'You didn't, huh? Talk sense, Jenny! How about that envelope-opener?'

'I don't *know* what you *mean*.'

'You don't! Where were you last night, huh?'

Jenny Friend shrank back in her chair. 'I — I went out for a walk,' she stammered.

'Sure, you went out for a walk!' Clay mimicked. 'Left a little souvenir behind you, huh?'

Suddenly, from beneath his coat, he whisked out a blood-stained handkerchief.

4

It was wet, wrinkled and crumpled. Bloodstains were all over it, and the whole was an ugly, faded, streaky brown. Clay's stubby forefinger rested on the embroidered 'F' in one corner.

'I reckon the game's up, Jenny,' said the inspector softly. 'There's your identification ticket. Now, understand, nobody's accusing you of croaking Embrich. What we want to know is, what happened when you and Vintner came here last night.'

'I wasn't here last night, I tell you!'

'Didn't see Vintner last night? Maybe you didn't go for that walk with him?'

'I won't answer you! I have a right — '

'Sure, Jenny, you've got every right.'

Jenny was staring fixedly at the hideous relic of the night's work. She appeared to be upon the verge of collapse. 'That — isn't — mine, anyway. I — never — saw — it — before,' she muttered.

'Come, come, Jenny, what's the sense

of lyin' like that?' asked Clay in gentle monition. 'Think you can get away with a tale like that? You're a thundering good ingénue actress, but a damn poor crook, to stuff that down the waste-pipe. And you're an accessory before the fact in Mr. Embrich's murder, anyway!' he thundered. 'I'm trying to make this just as easy as I can for you. So, unless you think you're as guilty as Vintner is, you'd better come across with it.'

The girl sprang to her feet, her face working convulsively. 'I tell you, I don't *know* anything about it, and that's *not* my handkerchief!' she cried. 'You *fool*; don't you know it's the first name that's embroidered for an initial, and not the last one?'

'Well, maybe the fashion's changed,' Clay retorted with acerbity. 'It doesn't matter to me if you want to take that line. Only, don't think we don't know who you're protecting. I guess there's someone else besides Vintner behind this affair, Jenny.'

The girl shuddered and turned her face away, staring out the window again. Jones began to understand the drift of the inspector's suspicions.

'When'd you last see Mr. Embrich, Jenny?' asked Clay.

'Yesterday afternoon,' she muttered.

'Was that before Mr. Goodloe had his quarrel with him, or after?'

'Before. He called me in to take some stenography.'

'You knew about the quarrel, then?'

'I knew Mr. Goodloe and Mr. Embrich had an argument.'

'When did you last see Mr. Goodloe?'

'I can't remember. Two or three weeks, perhaps.'

'Went joy-riding with him?'

'He took me out in his car.'

'Who told Vintner about it?'

'Why, Vintner didn't know it!' exclaimed the girl. 'It was Mr. Embrich he was angry about. Somebody had been spreading lies about me and him.'

'Lies, were they?' asked the inspector quietly. 'And why didn't they spread those lies about you and Mr. Goodloe?'

'How should I know? I only went out with Mr. Goodloe three times, anyway.'

'And Vintner was angry with Mr.

Embrich because someone lied about *you*! What did he have to say about it?'

'*I* didn't listen,' the girl snapped back. 'I've got too much to think about to worry what people say about me.'

'I guess you have!' responded Clay grimly. 'So Vintner was the friend you went walking with last night, eh, Jenny?'

The girl, momentarily confused by the question, turned her face away again. She resumed her sullen manner. 'I'm not going to answer any more questions,' she muttered.

'Well, I guess we've got all we want,' Clay answered. He turned to Myers. 'Keep her here till I arrange for her,' he said. 'I'll get a man down here to take charge of the papers.'

Clay left the room and entered Embrich's office. Jones heard him speaking softly at the telephone. Then there was a slight commotion in the gallery. A middle-aged man with a pointed beard and gold spectacles appeared, carrying a bag. He glanced sharply about him. Inspector Clay came out of the office and hurried to meet him.

'Good morning, sir,' he said. 'You'll

find — him — in this office.'

The medical examiner nodded and entered Embrich's room. He surveyed the inanimate form, bending over the wound, clucking and shaking his head. 'There'll have to be an autopsy. However, I'll make my preliminary examination.'

Clay withdrew and shut the door. He rubbed his thick hands together and turned to Jones with a pleased smile. 'Well, I guess things'll start humming pretty soon,' he remarked. 'There's only one point worrying me. Seems sort of queer Vintner was wise to the fact about Mr. Embrich taking a fancy to Jenny, and didn't know that Philip Goodloe had been taking her joy-riding.'

The door of Miss Martin's office opened and Rosanna came out, leading the secretary by the arm. Miss Martin turned and faced Clay.

'Listen to me, Inspector,' she exclaimed in ringing tones. 'I'll swear Mr. Goodloe had no hand in this affair. He isn't the sort of man you seem to take him for. He's just a thoughtless boy. He's taken a lot of girls out in his car, and it never meant a thing to him!'

'You seem to think a great deal of him, Miss Martin,' said Clay, surveying her white face.

'I do. Philip Goodloe isn't a murderer. He's not the sort of man who puts his best foot forward. But he's innocent.'

'You think Vintner and Jenny worked this alone, then?' Clay queried.

'Why, of course it was Vintner! Who else could it be? I don't know anything about the girl. Set Philip free! Don't hold him just because he insulted you when he was all broken down by the shock of learning of his uncle's death!'

Clay replied, 'When we know the exact time of the murder, after the medical examiner hands in his report, maybe Mr. Goodloe will be able to provide an alibi. But look at it the other way. Who else would've poisoned Vintner's mind against Mr. Embrich? Who else had as strong a motive? Who else stood to profit in the same way by his death? It wasn't only yesterday they quarreled, either. It was a problem of long-standing. Mr. Goodloe must have been expecting to be cut out of his uncle's will ever since Miss Beach left home.' He went on: 'Well, Miss Martin, you understand me. I haven't said I think young Goodloe guilty. But I'll have to hold him, with those fingerprints against him. That's all I can say. And I guess you'd better go home now, Miss Martin.'

Rosanna led Miss Martin, now weeping silently, toward the gallery. Clay gave a sharp order to one of his men. 'Send 'em all home below,' he said. 'And shoot those newspapermen up quick. I'll see 'em all — *now!*'

Rosanna came slowly back. She stopped at the inspector's side. 'Inspector, you — you didn't happen to find the thing that had been used to scour the floor beneath Mr. Embrich's desk, did you?' she asked. 'I mean a — an embroidered handkerchief.'

Clay stared at Rosanna in amazed surprise. 'Why, what makes you think — ' he began; and then, as Rosanna seemed to insist, he grimly produced the hideous trophy. 'I guess you've got a right to see it, since you're Mr. Jones's partner,' he answered. 'It don't happen to be yours, Miss Beach, does it? If not, how the thundering dickens did you — '

She turned it over in her fingers, inspecting it carefully. She looked at the embroidered 'F', held it up to the light, then let the handkerchief fall. A tremor ran through her frame and, with a deep sigh, she sank in a dead faint into Jones's arms.

★ ★ ★

In a few moments Rosanna opened her eyes, stared at the circle of faces round her, and sat up. Jones, who was being besieged by the newspapermen, to whom he was no stranger, saw Clay helping the girl solicitously to her feet, while watching her with a singular expression. The inspector stooped and picked up the handkerchief which had fallen to the floor, and placed it inside his coat.

'I guess this morning's work has been too much for Miss Beach,' he said to Jones, who, anxious to protect the girl from unnecessary inquiries, had broken through the circle and gone to her side. 'You'd better see her to her home,' he added.

'No,' said Rosanna, 'I'm going back to the office.'

'But, Miss Beach — ' Jones began in protest.

'I'm quite all right now, Mr. Jones, and I prefer to go back to work,' insisted Rosanna, closing her mouth in a tight, obstinate line.

Supporting the girl by the arm — he would have put his own arm round her waist to help her if he had dared — he conducted her down the stairs and out of the now deserted store. Unnoticed by the still gaping throng, who no doubt imagined them to be employees, he succeeded in fighting a passage through the mob and, Rosanna obstinately refusing to let him summon a taxicab, they boarded one of the trolley-cars, and soon reached the office.

'The inspector was quite right; you really ought to have gone home,' said Jones, looking anxiously at the girl's white face, as Rosanna sat back in her chair.

'Would you mind getting me a glass of water, please?' asked Rosanna faintly.

Jones hurried to the filter at the head of

the stairs. When he came back with his customary hurried stride he saw Rosanna standing on a chair, one hand stretched up toward two bulky tomes on the top shelf. The girl started nervously as she saw him. The chair began to topple. Rosanna clutched at the bookshelves, and Jones just managed to save her from a nasty fall.

He looked up at the two volumes on which her hand had rested. 'Miss Beach, you're positively the finest little worker I've ever known!' he said in admiration. 'Fancy your starting in so soon, after your experiences this morning! And you went straight to the mark! I didn't know you had ever heard of Boyle's *Inquiry into the Laws of Averages*. Unnecessarily drawn out, perhaps, and, his *Theorem on Mortality* has become obsolete since we have had the collected actuaries' reports; still, there is no doubt that Boyle was, in a particular sense, the father of the science of probability.

'Now, I don't believe that Boyle's researches would throw any particular light on the present case,' Jones continued, warming to his subject. 'However, if you were thinking of examining Boyle, I'll get those volumes down for you.' He moved toward the bookshelves. Rosanna's exclamation had in it a note of almost hysterical alarm.

'No, *no* — *please, Mr. Jones!*' she exclaimed. 'I don't — don't care to see them. As a matter of fact, I was simply examining a few of the titles.'

She drank a few sips of the water, while Jones studied her with his fatherly appreciation, showing much concern. 'Well, I suppose it's no use trying to get rid of you, Miss Beach!' he said. 'I know you won't be satisfied until you have cleared Mr. Goodloe.'

'Indeed I shall *not!*' the girl responded. 'Of course, I feel the shock very deeply, and I'm afraid I didn't keep my self-control very well.'

'You did splendidly!' answered Jones. 'See anything?'

'Uh-huh!' said Rosanna noncommittally. 'But the shock of finding Uncle Cy dead, and then of Philip's arrest, sort of threw me out of gear. When you said there was a murder coming, how little I guessed it would be poor Uncle Cy!'

'You'd have been more than human if you hadn't felt that way,' said Jones. 'But how did you know there was a handkerchief?'

'I — just inferred it,' answered Rosanna. 'And you know, Mr. Jones, it was always understood between us that I was to work on the clues while you do the mathematical part.'

'Quite right! Of course, I know that you like to get all your clues together before taking them up with me. And I'm such a dunderhead on observation, as I think you were observing only this morning. But still, I must say I was absolutely staggered by that deduction of yours. I guess Clay was staggered, too — I never saw him look so flabbergasted.'

Rosanna smiled wearily.

'And, by the way,' Jones went on, 'I must say I was surprised when he upset that pail of water. It almost looked to me — I was just behind him — as if he did it on purpose.'

'On purpose?' echoed Rosanna. 'Why, what do you — ?' She broke off, and a look which was unmistakably fear came upon her face for a moment.

'Well, of course I know he didn't,' Jones continued. 'But Clay's usually so restrained in all his movements. However — what is your theory, Miss Beach?'

'I don't know yet,' answered Rosanna in a grave tone. 'Yes, I did pick up a clue or two, Mr. Jones, and I'm going to lay them before you just as soon as they've led me anywhere. But I admit I'm puzzled.'

'I told you, you will remember, that the murder which was due would be of a startling character. Now there's a love element in it. And yet it isn't a love murder. You don't believe it's Vintner?'

'I'm sure it isn't,' answered Rosanna. She hesitated a moment. 'Mr. Jones — ' she began softly.

A more observant man might have detected a note in the girl's voice indicative of the desire to make some statement of a confidential nature; Jones, of course, was deaf to it. He went on: 'You've no idea as yet who it was?'

Rosanna shrugged. 'Jenny Friend has had no more to do with it than I have,' she answered. 'Tell me what happened when you and Clay went into the room.'

Jones recounted the conversation in summary. 'You see,' he continued, 'Clay had found that handkerchief, and had been holding it to spring on her. That's what made him so startled when you asked him about it. You don't believe that's pretty strong proof against Jenny?'

'No,' answered Rosanna. 'No proof at all. It's the initial of the first name that's used on a handkerchief almost always.'

'Why, that's exactly what Jenny told Clay!' exclaimed Jones. 'Of course it's almost useless speculating who was the murderer until I've worked out my charts — and until we've had more evidence. I must say everything points dead to Vintner at the present. I'd believe he was the guilty party if it wasn't for that odd element being due in this present murder.'

'But you do believe that Philip had nothing to do with it, don't you?' pleaded Rosanna.

Jones spoke with hesitation. 'If it wasn't for his fingerprints — ' he began.

Rosanna picked up a slender paper-cutter that was lying among a heap of papers on Jones's desk. She balanced it in her hand. 'Just look at this a moment, Mr. Jones,' she said. 'You see that if I finger this in an absent-minded sort of way I leave my fingerprints anywhere upon the steel. But now I am grasping it firmly in my hand, as if I meant to stab you. Whether I intended to deliver the natural, underhand thrust which every murderer uses, or the overhand from the movies, which nobody ever used — because instinct tells him he would expose his side to a counterblow — you will notice that the fingertips, close, not on the cutter, but on the palm of the hand.

'With a blade as slender as this, or in Mr. Timson's paper-cutter, the part of the fingers that touches the blade is that immediately opposite the first joint, on the underside. Now look at your fingers. The characteristic lines and whorls are here represented, on your fingers, and mine, and everyone's, simply by straight clefts in the skin.

'I think the position of Mr. Goodloe's fingertips on the opener will be shown to be such that the imprint could not have been made when he was in the act of delivering a thrust.'

Jones studied the thing out. 'Miss Beach, you certainly are a miracle!' he exclaimed enthusiastically. 'As I said, without you all my theorizing would be useless. I can't imagine how I got along before you came.'

The girl smiled faintly; Jones saw that her face was still drawn and white. 'Miss Beach,' he said, 'I wonder if you had a good breakfast this morning. Did you?'

'Not very,' confessed Rosanna.

'Then,' said Jones decisively, 'I'm going to take you out to lunch. When we come back, we'll start on our case, and go into it in the only sure, legitimate way — according to the truths of probability.'

The girl, who had been thrusting a pin into her hat, stopped and, laying her hand upon her arm, looked up earnestly into his face.

'Mr. Jones, tell me one thing. You do believe now that Philip's innocent, don't you?'

'I do,' Jones answered with conviction. 'There's really not a shred of evidence against him, except that matter of the fingerprints. But there's no need to worry about him, Miss Beach,' he went on with equal earnestness. 'The charts will show. When we plot the lines and curves, it'll be demonstrated exactly.'

'Then,' Rosanna persisted, 'I can count on you to do everything in your power to establish Philip's innocence?'

'I promise you to leave no stone unturned,' Jones answered solemnly.

And, as he spoke, there came into his mind the picture of Goodloe and Rosanna together before the altar. He had already relegated his seven-percent chance of acceptance upon the third time to zero. He knew now that he could never again ask Rosanna to be his wife.

So he vowed with all his soul to clear Goodloe of suspicion and unite him to this girl who loved and wore his engagement ring.

5

When they returned nearly an hour later, the ring of the telephone greeted them. Rosanna, listening to Jones speaking, recognized Clay's booming voice as the other.

Jones listened a few moments and hung up the receiver. 'It's Clay,' he said. 'He wants us to meet him at Mr. Embrich's house. He's surprisingly cordial — quite different from the way I found him on that last case, when he seemed so suspicious of my methods.'

They went out and took an uptown car. The Embrich house was a large brownstone building: large, but not handsome, and in no way distinguishable from its neighbors. It conveyed the impression of prosperity. The two were admitted by a heavy-featured, rather somber-looking butler who surveyed them in a furtive and gloomy manner.

Almost immediately behind him Clay

appeared, standing in the dark hallway. 'Afternoon, Mr. Jones,' said the inspector cordially. 'The same to you, Miss Beach. I didn't expect to trouble you so soon, but I'm anxious for us all to work together on this case.

'Peck here is a new man, I understand,' he continued. 'I guess you couldn't have seen him before, Miss Beach. Mr. Embrich engaged him only a couple of weeks ago in place of the old one, I understand, who got a better job. Well, Peck tells me that some woman telephoned the house about half past nine last night, asking if she could talk to Mr. Embrich. I hadn't heard anything about it before. You ask Peck here what he's got to tell about it.'

'Did she leave her name?' inquired Rosanna.

'No, miss, she refused to give it.'

'What did she ask you? Can you remember her words exactly?'

'She wanted to know if she could talk to Mr. Embrich. That's about all she said, miss. I told her Mr. Embrich was staying late at the store, and she said she'd go down there at once to see him, and hung up the receiver.'

He glanced at Clay when he had finished speaking, and Jones fancied that some sort of almost imperceptible signal passed between the two men.

'Anythin' more you want to ask him, Miss Beach?' the inspector queried, as Rosanna remained silent.

'I don't think so. Having been so short a time with my uncle, he wouldn't likely know anything material,' said Rosanna. 'I suppose he hasn't any knowledge or — or suspicions about Mr. Embrich's death? My uncle had no enemies of whom you have heard?' she continued to Peck.

'No, miss.'

'Thank you, Peck. That'll be all,' said Clay. He turned to the others. 'Well, we've kept things hummin' since this morning,' he said. 'Suppose we go into the library for a few minutes, and I'll try to update you.'

They proceeded along the passage into a room at the back, a gloomy place despite the large windows, through which the light straggled down from between the high buildings around. There was a Turkish carpet on the floor, the furniture was mahogany and massive, and the glistening leather of well-bound books added to the general atmosphere of elegance.

Clay waved Jones and Rosanna to seats, as if the place were his. Jones, who never smoked, declined the cigar offered him, and Clay bit off the end of it and lit it.

'Well, Mr. Jones,' he began, 'I'm givin' you the straight goods. It's not usual for the force to cooperate in this way, of course. But it suits me, and I guess there's more ways than one in which we can help each other. So you'll be kept posted to the dot, Mr. Jones, and anytime you want anything from headquarters — why, it's yours for the asking!'

'In that case I guess we'll make a pretty clean job of this affair.'

Clay shot a keen glance at him, almost as if he wondered whether there was any irony in Jones's remark. His survey of Jones's honest face seemed to reassure him. 'You're on!' he answered. 'Glad to find we can work harmoniously. You haven't doped out anything yet, I suppose?'

'I haven't got busy yet,' said Jones, 'though I may say that I know, from my previous investigations, that certain elements are present which should make our investigations relatively simple. I'll be glad to show you at my office as soon as you find it convenient to come.'

'I'll be there,' responded Clay promptly. 'Look you up tomorrow, maybe. We're scouring the city to find Vintner, and I'm expecting to hear we've got him most any hour now. It looks like Vintner and Jenny plain enough, and they pulled off the job before Mann had locked the Fothergill Street door.'

'Then — Mr. Goodloe?' asked Rosanna earnestly. 'You can't believe — '

'Now don't you worry about him, Miss Beach. Just as soon as we've got hold of Vintner everything'll come out. But, you see, if I was to let him go, with his prints on that envelope-opener, and anything happened later, pointing to him as an accessory — well, it'd mean my head! You see that, don't you?' Clay's voice had in it a soft, conciliatory deference that appeared unusual. There was, however, a catlike quality in

Clay, for all his brusqueness; that same hinting at secret knowledge which made him a terror.

Rosanna's eyes met Clay's in a long, steady look. Fearlessly the girl seemed to accept the inspector's challenge to do battle on behalf of the man she loved. For half a minute the two protagonists confronted each other, Rosanna's face set rigidly, Clay's suave and insinuating, although his eyes were steel.

Clay turned to Jones. 'We've got the medical examiner's preliminary report, and he says the murder must have happened between ten and eleven last night. That'd have left her plenty of time to get down to the store — if it was Jenny.'

Rosanna interrupted: 'Mann said that he locked the Fothergill Street door at 9:45.'

'Between that time and ten. Didn't seem certain,' Clay corrected. 'As to that, I guess the old fellow naturally wanted to put the best light on the door having been left open, and so we'll allow he locked up somewhere between ten and a quarter past. Say the job was pulled off a few minutes after ten! That leaves us plenty of time.

'Second,' continued Clay, with a note of exultation in his voice, 'we've got another clue, which was found almost as soon as you'd left the store. It's a woman's hair, and it was found on Mr. Embrich's shoulder. This hair was on the shoulder nearest the window, and the woman who owned it leaned over Mr. Embrich's neck.'

Clay leaned back and stretched out his legs. 'Of course, that don't prove it was Jenny who stabbed Mr. Embrich,' he continued, 'and for my part I don't believe she did. But no doubt she saw the job done, and I guess she and Vintner'll loosen up between them now, and we'll be able to get at the facts.'

'I suppose that Miss Friend's room has been searched?' Jones queried.

'What for?' growled Clay, who seemed rather taken aback by the question.

'Why, to find if she had any more handkerchiefs like that one that was discovered at the store. And then there's those rubbers with the circles on the soles that you were speaking about.'

Clay's face resumed its sardonic mask. 'I reckon you think there's a doubt about Jenny,' he answered. 'Well, we're not exactly greenhorns or amateurs in the police department, Mr. Jones.

'Jenny's room was searched, and I admit we found nothing doing along either of those two lines. But that makes no hit with me, because, I guess Jenny had sense enough to hide her tracks after she got home. It was her feelin's after she'd seen Mr. Embrich murdered before her eyes that made her fool enough to try to clean the floor with her handkerchief, and then to stuff it in the waste-pipe, thinkin' it wouldn't be found there. And as for the rubbers — why, that pattern's not rare enough to help us. They're selling 'em at most of the stores. That leads nowhere.'

'And what about the lilies?' Jones inquired.

'Lilies? Oh, yes.' Clay was silent for a moment. 'Well, I give it up. I cannot fathom the reason for them just now. They're selling lilies in the shops everywhere this time of the year.

86

'Well, I guess I've put you wise now, Mr. Jones,' he continued, getting up heavily. 'It's a clear trail, and when we've got Vintner you'll see that it's him and Jenny. And then, Miss Beach, Mr. Goodloe'll have every chance to show he had nothing to do with it.'

He opened the door for Rosanna. The three passed out. As Jones and the girl were about to descend the steps, Clay called to them. 'I've been thinkin' over that little discrepancy between Mann's evidence and the medical examiner's opinion,' he said. 'I'd like to get Mann to admit he locked that door a little later than he thought he did. It's not of the first importance, but it'd straighten out a little kink if he changed his mind by a few minutes. I guess I'll run out to Flatbush tonight and have a talk with him. I'll pick you up in the car at the bridge entrance about eight.'

★　★　★

A fairly long drive through Flatbush brought them to Mann's house. It proved

87

to be a tiny, ancient, rather dilapidated wooden building standing in a little weedy garden, and surrounded by waste fields producing scrub-growth and rusty wire in almost equal proportions.

A tousled-haired boy with locks as red as a carrot, and an honest grin that put an extra dent in his snub nose, opened the door. Clay wore plainclothes, but the boy stood to attention like a policeman.

'Hello, kid!' exclaimed the inspector. 'I didn't know this was your beat.' Clay looked from the grinning boy to Jones. 'This is the kid I get my evenin' paper from regular,' he said. 'So Daddy Mann's your father, is he?' he continued. 'I see the resemblance now. If you're a good lad we'll make a good policeman of you someday,' he added. 'Maybe you've got some brothers, too?'

'Nope. There never was nobody but me and sis,' answered the boy.

'So you've got a sister, eh? Where does she work?' asked Clay.

'I dunno. She don't live here no more,' returned the boy. A stubborn look came on his face.

'Well, suppose you tell your father there's a lady and two gentlemen to see him,' he suggested.

'Dad ain't in. He's gone with Mom to the meeting.'

'Well, I guess we can wait for them. Won't be long, I suppose?' said Clay, leading the way into the shanty. 'So your sister's out working now?' he inquired. 'Where does she live?'

'I dunno nothin' about her,' answered the boy stubbornly. 'I guess Pop put her out for good last summer. Ma's awful sore about it. I can hear her cryin' in the night sometimes, when Pop ain't snorin'.'

'That's a pity,' said Clay, drawing the inevitable conclusion as to the reason — at least, he showed no disposition to ask it. He made a slow circuit of the room, examining the furniture and pictures with apparent interest. 'I guess your dad brought these from the old country?' he asked, waving his hand toward the portrait of Queen Victoria.

'Aw, Pop's a back number,' answered the boy scornfully. 'I guess he thinks we Americans are still a British colony. I'll tell you what the trouble is,' he went on confidentially. 'He comes here too old. Why, I was born on the ship they sailed on, and I'm thirteen last January. Pop's sixty-five, and Mom's nearly sixty. Ain't it a shame to have an old pair like that for your family?'

Clay scowled. 'That's no way to talk of your father and mother, son,' he answered.

'Well, I didn't mean nothin'. But honest, they're too old to have any fun left in 'em. All they think about's going to prayer-meetings. I guess Dad was always that way, only he's got worse of late. But Mom wasn't. At least, I can remember when she wasn't. Now she's got as bad as Dad.'

'See here, son, you've got a mighty good father,' said Clay, 'and I guess your mother's a pretty good woman. And the quicker you follow in their tracks, the sooner you'll be fit to make a good man of yourself.'

'Well, I think it's a shame the way they put Dolly out of the house just because she liked fun better than goin' to prayer-meetin's,' said the lad obstinately.

'I told Pop straight I'd take my religion Sundays, and, if he didn't like it, I was payin' me way anyhow. Gee, Pop got mad! I guess he'd have put me out, too, only Mom wouldn't stand for it. 'You put one child out of your home instead of saving her,' she said, 'and this one's mine. He's mine, and he stays!' she says. And when Mom gets that kind of fit, what she says goes.'

'*Humph!*' snorted Clay in some disgust. 'I guess it's a good ways from here to the bridge. If I'd thought of it, Mr. Jones, we might have stopped there and looked up Mann at his meeting, instead of comin' all this way.'

'Why, Pop ain't at the bridge meetin'!' exclaimed the boy. 'He and Mom don't go there no more. They've got a new meetin' place on Avenue Q, just round the corner.'

'No sense waiting here,' grumbled Clay.

They went out. Rosanna, who had not come into the room, joined them. The boy followed them to the garden gate. 'It's over there,' he said. 'You can hear the meetin' if you listen hard.'

They listened. *Boom! Boom!* came the

faint sound of a beaten drum.

'Come on!' said Clay, jumping unceremoniously into the machine. 'We'll pull up a block away. I reckon those Salvationists might be scared if we were to drive right into 'em and yank Mann out by the hair.'

The increasing noise of drum and cymbals guided them. They stopped at the corner, and walked to an empty lot nearby. It was an outdoor service, conducted for the benefit of those who owned the few jerry-built shanties dumped here and there about the waste. As they approached, they saw Mann standing beside a preacher. Beside Mann stood a tiny old woman in a shawl and black bonnet with a harassed, lined, motherly face, now rapt in enthusiasm.

The preacher finished his harangue a few minutes after the arrival of the party and, after a hymn, the meeting began to disperse. Clay waited till Mann and his wife came face to face with him. Then he put his hand on the watchman's shoulder. Mann looked up calmly and recognized him.

'Pretty enthusiastic meeting you folks have been holding, Mann,' he said.

'Yes, sir.' Mann looked inquiringly out of his very bright, dark eyes.

'Just ran out your way to ask you something I didn't get quite straight this morning. Fine little place you have out here.' He beamed at the old lady. 'And that's a bright boy of yours, Mann. Many a time I've bought my evening paper from him, and never knew who he was. He'll be making the force one of these days, I guess. And, when he's ready, just send him along to me.'

'Yes, sir,' said Mann. 'He's smart enough, and he'll make a good man when he's got more sense in him, if he doesn't get led astray.'

'Bob's a good boy,' said the old woman.

'I'm sure of it, ma'am,' responded Clay heartily. 'I've had my eye on him, like most of the youngsters I see, and I saw he had the makings of a good man in him, as well as of a good policeman. Though, to my way of thinkin', there's not much difference between them.' Clay was plainly speaking from his heart. But then the sardonic mask that he had removed came back upon his face as he asked: 'You haven't another child, Mann, I suppose?'

'I have one child, and but one,' answered Mann, with a sudden, harsh quaver in his voice.

''tis not so!' cried the little old woman, with surprising vehemence. ''tis not so. A mother *neffer* forgets her child. A mother *neffer* casts her off. A mother's mind can *neffer* forget. A mother's heart is with *all* the childer she's bore.'

'I have but one child, and I know of *only* one,' repeated Mann stubbornly. 'What is dead to me is *dead*.'

'Dead to you, but *not* to me!' exclaimed his wife with intense bitterness. She turned back to Clay. 'Sir, I'll tell you,' she began. 'He drove his daughter from his house — yes, sir, his daughter, her that had been his heart's pride, because she made a false step, driven to it by a father's harshness.'

'Enough!' said Mann fiercely. His eyes gleamed with cold anger.

''tis not enough, and neffer shall be enough, husband! Had he given her his love as he gave it to the Lord, she would neffer have done what she did, sir. Stubborn, wrathful, and doubting, how shall you stand before your Maker at the last day and say, 'I drove her forth'?'

Clay thought it time to intervene, for the quarrel seemed to be flaring up still more fiercely. 'Well, Mrs. Mann, these family troubles are hard,' he said. 'Most of us have them. But I wanted to speak to your husband about Mr. Embrich. It must have been a shock to you when you learned of his death.'

'It was more than that,' said the old woman, her quiet, motherly manner returning. 'Mr. Embrich was the best man who ever lived whateffer.'

Jones recalled that Mann had said almost that identical thing in the office that morning.

She rubbed her frayed sleeve-end over her old, wrinkled eyes. 'Aye, the world's a queer place, sir,' she said, 'and sometimes I've wondered whether it mightn't be the hell we're told about, and us not knowing it.'

'*Hush*, wife!' said Mann. He turned to

the inspector. 'What was it that you wished to ask me about, sir?' he inquired.

'Why, Mann, you didn't answer one of my questions quite correctly this morning,' answered Clay. 'There's pretty strong reason to suppose you didn't lock that Fothergill Street door at half past ten yesterday night. And maybe you didn't lock it at all, but only imagined you did.'

'By the Big Man — ' began the watchman in a high tone of voice.

Clay cut him short. 'Now, understand me,' he interrupted. 'It don't amount to much, only we've got to get this point properly cleaned up, if we're to get our evidence in correctly. And I know you're anxious to do everything you can to bring the murderer to justice. So think again, Mann, and if you come to the conclusion that you didn't lock that door just at the time you thought you did — why, it won't make any difference as far as you're concerned. I'll just have to correct my report, that's all.'

Mann admitted that it *might* have been as late as a quarter after ten, because he did not remember having looked at his watch at the time. That seemed to satisfy Clay. He allowed the old couple to depart upon their homeward way. They watched them gesticulating at each other as they walked. It was clear that the old quarrel had fired up again as hotly as ever.

'Well, the — damned — old — cuss!' said Clay softly. 'He don't look it! Who'd have believed it? I can see now how the kid got his distaste for *that* brand of religion.'

He drove Jones and Rosanna back to town, dropping the girl at the door of her apartment. After a friendly 'good night' he was about to re-enter his car when Jones asked him: 'By the way, Inspector, now that the time of the murder's definitely known, surely it should be possible for Mr. Goodloe to show where he was between the hours of ten and eleven last night? Unless you claim that he was only remotely an accessory — and I understand you're holding him because of the fingerprints — such proof ought to set him at liberty.'

The look on Clay's face was more contemptuously sardonic than usual. 'He says he went for a walk,' Clay jeered. 'Just a little stroll round the town. Met nobody he knew, and didn't do nothin' in particular, except just walk. Now, what do you make of that?'

He climbed into his car and whirred away. Jones went to Rosanna, who was standing upon the doorstep, fingering her key.

'Did you hear that?' he asked. 'What a pity it will be if Mr. Goodloe can't — '

'Oh, please — *please* — please don't say anything more about him, Mr. Jones!' exclaimed the girl hysterically.

And she put her key in the lock, opened the door, and disappeared inside, leaving Jones gaping at her speechlessly from the sidewalk.

6

Jones, who usually reached his office a few minutes before Rosanna, got down half an hour earlier the following morning, with the determination to put in some hard work upon the diagrams. He was both disappointed and disconcerted when, two or three minutes after he had hung up his hat, Clay walked straight in.

The inspector's face bore an expression of elation. 'Mornin', Mr. Jones,' he said. 'Just stopped here on my way to the precinct, and took my chances of findin' you in. You might be interested to know we've picked up Vintner. Picked him up quiet as a lamb as he was goin' into his apartment late last night. We've got a nice little bunch of burglar's tools he had in his room, includin' a skeleton key that opens the door between Miss Martin's room and Mr. Embrich's as slick and soft as milk. He's bein' held on a charge of having a burglar's kit, but I guess he knows what we want him for. Refuses to give any account of his movements night before last. Thought you might like to come along.'

Jones was not altogether comfortable at the prospect; his forte was his charts and diagrams; the business of man-hunting interested him principally in its theoretical aspect. However, there was nothing to do but accept, and he left the office with Clay, who restricted his remarks to a few pessimistic forecasts upon the subject of the weather until they were seated side by side in the street car.

Then Clay turned his gaze upon Jones. 'By the way,' he began, 'there's a new piece of evidence turned up this morning that may interest you. We found Mr. Embrich's will among his papers. It looks genuine enough; though, of course, that point'll have to be decided later. But you'd be surprised to know who he's left the bulk of his property to. Ever hear Miss Beach suggest that Mr. Embrich might be a *married man?*'

Jones was astounded. 'Why, of course I understood that he was a *bachelor!*' he answered.

'Same here. But you can never tell. That's where the old man fooled 'em. Most men have a woman in their lives that folks don't know about, and Mr. Embrich was one of 'em. Only he seems to have made her his wife. Miss Beach and Mr. Goodloe get his personal estate and the house between 'em, but the whole business and the property go, lock, stock and barrel to 'my dear wife, Adelaide.' Now who in thunder's Adelaide, I wonder?'

'Beats me,' said Jones laconically. 'But, of course,' he added, 'I know nothing about Mr. Embrich's private affairs whatever.'

'Well, of course, I'm in the same boat as to that,' Clay answered. 'It looks as if she's someone he had good reason for not telling about. Lord, it's a hell of a joke on Miss Martin!' He chuckled. 'I guess the old lady had her eye on Mr. Embrich, and his property, too, for all she seems so anxious for his nephew and Rosanna. Lord, it makes me laugh to think how old Embrich fooled the pack of 'em. But that ain't my business, unless it seems to have

101

some bearin' on the case. Comin' back to Mr. Embrich's wife, it's mighty queer she hasn't turned up, with every paper featurin' Mr. Embrich's murder.'

He lapsed into silence during the remainder of the journey. Descending from the car, they walked the short block to the station-house and were shown into the detectives' room, where they were joined by Cohen, the precinct captain, a middle-aged man with a hook-nose and a grizzled red mustache.

'Vintner been talkin'?' asked Clay.

'Not a word.'

Leaving Jones, the inspector went over to where Cohen sat and began whispering to him. Clay seemed emphatic, and Cohen nodded once or twice, and once glanced toward Jones. Shortly, Vintner made his appearance in charge of a policeman. He proved to be a thick-set, burly-looking fellow with a shock of lank black hair and a sneering, confident demeanor. When the escort was dismissed, he stood in the middle of the room grinning.

'Hello, Vintner!' Clay greeted him.

'Mornin', Inspector. Why, if that ain't my old friend you've brought along with you!' he jeered. 'Hope your eyesight's better, Mr. Jones. Say, you got a bum partner, Clay!'

'Cut it out, Vintner!' responded the inspector. 'I guess you know what I've come to see you about. Feel like doin' any talkin'?'

Vintner grinned at him with confident impudence. 'Well, I dunno,' he answered. 'Seein' it's an old friend like you, Inspector, I don't mind telling you one of your *dicks* planted that kit of tools he says he found in my room, and I guess *you know it*.'

'Stop your kiddin', Vintner,' said the inspector. 'I guess you know we ain't particularly interested in that kit of tools of yours. We know you killed Mr. Embrich. We've got you cold, Vintner, and Jenny Friend's been talkin', too. Come through with it!'

Clay's voice was almost wheedling. Vintner threw back his head and laughed heartily; he appeared amused at Clay.

'This is where I've got you cold, Mr.

Clay,' he chuckled. 'I don't know nothin' about it, save what I read in the papers. I wasn't within a mile of Mr. Embrich's place all Tuesday.'

'That's a lie, Vintner. We've got a witness who saw you in the yard Tuesday afternoon,' said Clay.

Vintner's brows contracted. 'Say, if I thought you was speaking the truth, Inspector, I'd have something to tell you,' he answered. 'But I guess that's part of the game.'

'All right,' said Clay. 'Well suppose I'm lyin' then, and that you're innocent. You're the innocent victim, so you naturally want to clear yourself. And maybe you'd like to have that little matter of the kit dropped, too, in return for comin' through with somethin' of value. What's the objection?'

Vintner scowled viciously at Clay. 'I'll tell you what the *objection* is,' he barked. 'I ain't doin' any talkin' just now, except to say you got the wrong man. So you can do your own man-huntin' — you and your sidekick Jones here, who can't see across that long nose of his.'

'Have your fun, Vintner,' responded Clay placidly. 'You're not hurtin' us; you're hurtin' yourself. All you got to do is tell us where you were on Tuesday night, if you still think you're innocent. Or, if you've changed your mind about that — ' He leaned forward and transfixed Vintner with his gaze. ' — tell us what you know.'

Vintner laughed again. 'I don't mind tellin' you I was out walking with a lady friend,' he answered. 'I'll tell you more when I get ready — *maybe*.'

The perpetual answer certainly got on Clay's nerves. There was almost a snarl in the inspector's voice. 'That's all right, Vintner. We *know* you and Jenny were out walkin'.'

Vintner's nostrils dilated, and he seemed upon the verge of a furious answer; then, controlling himself, he uttered a malicious chuckle. 'I guess I can mind my own business, Mr. Clay,' he answered. 'I said I was out walkin' with a lady friend. I didn't say nothin' about Jenny.'

'But I'll tell you the rest, Vintner,'

responded Clay very softly. 'The answer where you walked to is, into Mr. Embrich's store by the Fothergill Street entrance. The door had been left unlocked, and we know all about that. You walked in, dodged the watchman, and went up the back stairs and along the passage. You opened Mr. Embrich's door with that bunch of keys that was found at your place. Mr. Embrich was workin' at his desk, or maybe he was takin' a wink or two. You stabbed him in the back like the coward you are, with that envelope-opener you'd got from Jenny!'

If it was Clay's plan to break Vintner down by this reconstruction of the crime, Clay certainly failed. Vintner's sneering smile had a distinct look of malicious triumph in it.

'After you'd done the job, Jenny got scared,' continued Clay. 'She hadn't known you meant to murder Mr. Embrich. She'd thought it was just one of the jobs you've been working on since you come out of the pen. She ran to him and tried to wipe the blood away. Then she saw that it was drippin' down on the

106

floor, and she got down and scrubbed the floor with her handkerchief. She stuffed it down the waste-pipe afterward. We've got the handkerchief, with her initial on it.

'Then she leaned over Mr. Embrich's body, and put her arms round his neck, and cried. You know, she was sweet on him, Vintner, even if she did arrange to pull off that job with you. She cared for him a hell of a lot more than she did for you. She left some of her hair on his shoulder. We've got the hair.

'Now, what I'm askin' you, Vintner, is this: whether you got nothin' to say that might maybe make it look like a possible second-degree murder. If you come through clean, maybe somethin' of the kind might be done for you. I'm not promisin', but if you don't come through, then the chair's waitin' for you, lad, as sure as you've been born.'

Vintner's lips parted in a wider sneer than before. 'My God,' he said huskily, 'my God, Clay, what a damn *liar* you are!'

Clay's great fist doubled; it looked for the moment almost as if he meant to strike the prisoner. Captain Cohen leaned forward and touched him on the shoulder.

'You've had your chance, and it don't come twice,' he answered, pressing the buzzer on the desk. 'Take him back!' he ordered the escort. 'See you outside, Mr. Jones,' he added casually.

For a moment Jones's eyes met Clay's. And it was impossible for Jones to mistake the look Clay gave him. The mask had fallen utterly from the inspector's face. Hate and hostility showed plain and unconcealed. It was the first time it had occurred to Jones that Clay's protestations of amity might be false. Very simple-minded, Jones always took men at their face value. He had put aside Rosanna's distrust of Clay as the illusion of an overwrought girl.

But what was at the bottom of Clay's actions? he wondered as he paced slowly up and down in front of the station-house. Was it all a colossal bluff? Was Vintner really innocent, and did Clay suspect it? Was he seeking evidence that would send Goodloe, and not Vintner, to the chair? Why was he playing this game

— if it was a game — with him?

He could not answer his own questions, but he resolved to be on his guard thenceforward. Instinct, which seldom spoke to him, spoke (when it did) with the force of an imperative mandate. He resolved to play his own hand in the future.

And as he was about to start homeward he saw Clay coming out of the station-house. 'Hold your horses!' said the inspector, hurrying up to him. 'Which way were you going? I thought maybe you'd like to come back to headquarters and see Miss Martin. I had her telephoned about that will of Embrich's, asking her to come down and see if she could identify the signature.'

Jones decided to accompany him. Rosanna knew what she had to do, and was doubtless already at work.

At headquarters, however, Jones found Miss Martin *and* Rosanna waiting in the outer office of the homicide bureau. The inspector nodded, asked them to wait a few minutes, and went inside.

Rosanna came up to Jones. 'Miss

Martin came down to the office just after I arrived,' she said. 'They had telephoned for her, and then she had a visit from Detective Myers, which upset her so much that she came to your office first to ask your advice. I thought it best to come over here with her.'

Miss Martin came up to them. 'I'm so relieved to see you, Mr. Jones,' she said. 'Isn't it dreadful, about Mr. Embrich's will! You've heard about it, haven't you?' She looked at Jones with burning eyes. Her face was drawn, like an old woman's.

'Inspector Clay mentioned it to me this morning,' Jones answered.

'I had a telephone call while I was dressing, asking me to come down here, and I couldn't make head or tail of it,' said the secretary. 'That will can't be genuine,' she went on agitatedly. 'Why, I never heard of any woman called Adelaide, and I never dreamed Mr. Embrich was married! I always felt perfectly certain he'd divide his money and property equally between Rosanna and Philip. You poor dear,' she added to Rosanna. 'It must have been a dreadful shock to you!'

'I never heard of such a woman, either,' said Rosanna. 'If my uncle has married a decent woman, who was worthy of him, I'm sure the money's nothing at all to me.'

'But I say it's *incredible*,' said Miss Martin, with rising vehemence, 'that Mr. Embrich could have been acquainted with any woman I'd never heard of — that is, sufficiently to ask her to become his wife. I was in the closest touch with all his private affairs for years. And then, even if he had married her, to think of his leaving her the entire business, with that immensely valuable property! Why, Rosanna, you and Philip are both practically disinherited, except for the house on Sixty-Ninth Street and the few thousands Mr. Embrich has to his credit in the bank! And poor Philip's never done anything since he lost that importing business that Mr. Embrich started him in years ago. Who is this Adelaide whom nobody has ever heard of?'

'I'm absolutely certain that Uncle Cy never knew such a woman when I was living with him,' Rosanna repeated. 'If there is such a person, she must have come into his life since then.'

'But if she really exists, wouldn't she have come, or telegraphed, if she's out of the state, the moment she read the news of Mr. Embrich's death?'

'She can't be in ignorance of it. Do you think it could be a — a sort of *joke*? You know Uncle Cy was fond of joking.'

'He never joked about money,' cried Miss Martin. She turned to Jones. 'What do you think about it?' she asked hysterically.

'I should say that it's not much use speculating about it until we know whether the will's genuine,' answered Jones. 'If she exists, she may be ill, or living in some country place and not have seen the New York papers.'

'But I can't wait! It's too *terrible*!' the secretary exclaimed, wringing her hands and beginning to pace up and down the floor. 'And that poor boy in that dreadful cell! It breaks my heart to think of him. Perhaps Philip has heard of the woman. Rosanna, we must go to him! They can't refuse us. Everybody must see that it was

Vintner who murdered Mr. Embrich! Who *else* could it be?'

She almost screamed the last words, and suddenly collapsed into her chair again. Her figure was huddled like a child's. Rosanna kneeled beside her, hushing the wild outburst upon her lips. 'He didn't do it! I'll tell all the world if need be!' Jones heard the girl saying. 'It only means that they'll probably hold Philip a day or two.'

'If we could only prove where Mr. Goodloe was at the time of the murder — ' Jones suggested tentatively, awkwardly conscious of the keen observation of the two policemen present.

'Where he was? He went out for a walk. He always took a little stroll late at night. It made him sleep!' declared Miss Martin.

Rosanna seemed almost as distracted as the older woman. Jones saw Miss Martin clutch at her and pull her head down. She whispered fiercely in her ear. He saw Rosanna nod. 'Yes, it's best not to try to see him now. Yes, if it comes to that,' he heard the girl declare. And then Miss Martin was on her feet again, coherent, calm, pressing

113

her handkerchief to her eyes.

They became aware that the door of the inner office had opened, and Clay stood in the entrance beckoning to them. They went in, and closed the door softly. 'Sit down, Miss Martin,' he said, offering her a chair. 'I'm sorry you're so distressed. It's natural, of course, quite natural. Now, we found what purports to be Mr. Embrich's will among his private papers. Here it is. Would you and Miss Beach be inclined, at first sight, to say that signature's genuine?'

He placed the will before them. It was written on a single sheet of stationery, signed, and witnessed. Miss Martin took it in her hand and read it through. 'I've never heard of either of those men before,' she said, placing her finger upon the names of the witnesses at the bottom of the paper.

Clay raised his eyebrows. 'But the *signature*, Miss Martin — the signature,' he said. 'In your opinion, is it that of Mr. Embrich, or isn't it?'

'It may be his, or it may be a forgery,' Miss Martin began, 'I can't swear — '

'Nobody's askin' you to swear, Miss Martin. That's a matter for the court. All I'm askin' you is whether you think it's Mr. Embrich's signature or whether you don't. Come, you must know Mr. Embrich's signature better than anyone, havin' seen it every day for years past!'

'It is either Mr. Embrich's signature, or else a very clever forgery,' said Miss Martin, speaking very slowly and deliberately.

'That's better, Miss Martin. And how about yourself, Miss Beach?' he added, turning toward Rosanna and placing the will upon the table in front of her.

Rosanna, after studying the signature carefully, answered: 'I believe it's genuine. I know my uncle's signature so well.'

'Thanks. Sorry to have had to press you ladies,' said Clay. 'But the reason I asked is that I've had a — '

As he spoke his telephone rang. With an exclamation of impatience he snatched the receiver, listened a moment, and put it back. He got up and strode to the door, flinging it open. Outside stood a policeman accompanied by a pretty, fashionably dressed woman of not more than thirty. She seemed in as much distress as Miss Martin had been. She, too, was holding a handkerchief to her eyes, and dabbing at them as she was conducted toward the door of Clay's office. As Clay appeared upon the threshold she took the handkerchief away and tried to speak, but could only sob helplessly.

The policeman handed Clay a card with something scribbled on it. Clay looked at it, then at the girl, said something softly to her, and, taking her by the arm, led her inside and closed the door again.

'The reason I asked,' continued the inspector, as if there had been no interlude, 'is that I've got a hunch this is goin' to concern everybody. Take a chair, Miss Orr.'

But the girl, as if unconscious of the presence of anyone else, turned to Clay and put two small, well-gloved hands upon his coat sleeve.

'Won't you tell me if it's true — about Mr. Embrich having been murdered?' she panted. 'They sent me here to see you. They wouldn't tell me a word. I can bear it if it's true — it's everyone refusing to answer me that's driving me mad.'

'It's true enough, Miss Orr, I'm sorry to say — been in all the papers since yesterday's noon editions,' Clay responded.

The girl, recoiling at his affirmation, stood leaning back against the wall, her hands pressed to her bosom. 'I — I can't *believe* it!' she gasped. 'It doesn't sound possible. *Murdered?*'

Clay inclined his head. 'Mr. Embrich was stabbed to death in his office on Tuesday night,' he answered. 'He died instantaneously.'

'And the — the funeral — ?'

'This afternoon. I'll see you're notified. Sit down, Miss Orr, and pull yourself together.' He led her to a chair, and the girl sat down as if dazed.

She looked up at him, her large, gray eyes dilated in terror. 'Why should anyone have murdered him? Who was it?' she asked.

'That,' answered Clay with emphasis, and obvious sincerity, 'we'll find out soon — mighty soon, Miss Orr.'

'I only saw the headlines in the paper this morning as I was coming down to headquarters in the subway,' the girl sobbed. 'I'm an actress, and I came in from the road late last night. I've been touring in Connecticut. I was coming down here about the burglary. When I got home I found my apartment had been ransacked from end to end, and yet nothing taken, although there was some jewelry — only my things left strewn about the floor. This is the third time that's happened to me. I left my *last* apartment on account of it.

'On the way down in the train I started to read a paper I'd bought, and saw the headlines about Mr. Embrich being dead. I threw the paper away — I couldn't bear to look at it. When I gave my name at headquarters I only wanted to know about Mr. Embrich, and they wouldn't answer me. They insisted on sending me here to you.'

'Pardon my askin' it, Miss Orr, but what was Mr. Embrich to you?'

'He was a friend — a very *dear* friend. He — he — '

'You don't happen to be his *wife*, Miss Orr, do you?' persisted Clay. 'Ya see, his

118

will mentions his wife Adelaide, who inherits the bulk of his property. She didn't seem to be known to these two ladies, who represent Mr. Embrich's family, and we've been expectin' her to turn up. Adelaide's an uncommon name, and when you gave it in connection with Mr. Embrich here, we all naturally supposed that you might be the lady we were looking for.'

The girl's head drooped. 'Yes,' she answered wearily, 'it was to have been kept a secret for a little longer, but it doesn't matter now. Mr. Embrich was my husband. We were married in New Jersey two months ago, but it was not to have been announced until the termination of my engagement. Then everybody was to have been told. It seems now impossible for me to realize it ever happened.'

'Excuse my askin' you,' said Clay, 'but you have your certificate, of course?'

'Yes, at home. I'll bring it. I — '

Her head fell forward and she slipped, fainting, to the floor.

Clay glanced at Jones and Rosanna. 'I guess you'd better leave. Things are

119

getting a bit awkward here . . . I'll handle it when she recovers. I'll update you later.'

As Jones and Rosanna left, the latter turned and stared intently at the unconscious woman before following her employer out.

7

When Jones entered his office he found Rosanna there already, although it was very early in the morning. A glance showed him that she was hard at work upon the catalogue of murder variables, which pleased him mightily.

This was Friday. The murder had occurred Tuesday; already the papers had ceased to feature the news, relegating it to an inner page.

The funeral had taken place on the preceding afternoon. Rosanna had, of course, attended it, and Jones, left alone, and unwilling to tackle the variables without Rosanna, had spent most of the time in computations which had brought him to no very definite conclusion.

'I've finished, Mr. Jones,' said his assistant.

'What? Finished *already*?' demanded Jones in astonishment. 'What time did you get here, Miss Beach?'

'I came down at seven. You see, I was awfully anxious to get this job completed. And it was much quicker than I expected. There are eighty-five.'

'Eighty-five variables? Well, that's not many. I'm ashamed to have been loafing while you were working, Miss Beach, but — *only eighty-five?*'

'There would have been ninety-four if Miss Martin and I hadn't agreed that the signature of the will was genuine. I thought we'd eliminate the nine under the circumstances.'

'Quite right. Eighty-five variables, eh? Well, now we'll be able to go full steam ahead,' said Jones. 'This business sure does beat Creation. I guess Clay thinks so, too.'

Rosanna looked at him keenly. 'You mean he's not so sure it's Vintner and Jenny as he pretends?' she asked.

'I went with him yesterday morning to see him sweat Vintner,' answered Jones. 'Vintner called him a damn liar to his face. And Clay took it. Now what do you make of that? Clay's not the sort of man to do that unless — unless — Well, it wasn't altogether *that*, but he gave me a look just at that moment, that was a positive revelation to me. I had an intuition. Not that I believe in things like that. Give me pure mathematics. Only I remembered you said you distrusted him.'

'Intuition's a great deal *better* than mathematics! That's what I meant when I told you I didn't trust him,' said Rosanna. 'Inspector Clay is playing a deep game of his own. Why did he arrest Philip if he's so confident it's Vintner? Mr. Jones, he's *using* us — he's not *helping* us. You agree with me now?'

'I did think,' said Jones, 'that he was impressed by your inference about that handkerchief.'

Rosanna shook her head. 'I think you'll find that Inspector Clay's professed anxiety to work with us has about reached its end.'

The telephone rang. With a sickening premonition that his work was still to be delayed, Jones took down the receiver. After a short exchange, he covered it with his hand.

'It's Clay again,' he said. 'He wants to

know if he can come round and learn something of my methods. You know, we spoke about it. I'll tell him to come tomorrow.'

Rosanna shook her head violently. 'No, let him come — let him come *now*!' she whispered. 'We want him in the open!'

Jones obeyed her, and after minutes of strained suspense, Clay entered the little office. He took his seat in Jones's swivel-chair, by invitation, while Jones perched his ungainly body upon the edge of the desk.

'I guess I'm pesterin' you folks a good deal,' Clay began, 'but you aroused my interest considerable, Mr. Jones, the other day, when you spoke of certain elements existin' which ought to make our investigation simple. Of course it's simple, and I stick to my point that it's a clear case against Vintner and Jenny, leavin' Mr. Goodloe out of consideration for the present. But what have you doped out with those diagrams of yours?'

Jones bent over the desk and began searching among his papers which covered it. It was an amazing pile and, as a

124

mole throws debris while it works, Jones brought to light open books with the covers gone, scrawled paper slips, a handkerchief, a necktie, a stack of rent receipts, two quarters, and the hand-mirror from Rosanna's bag. Clay watched him in mild amusement, glancing once or twice with a raised eyebrow at Rosanna, who looked on with embarrassment.

'Here, take your chair!' said Clay, rising and pushing Jones into it, while he seated his massive form upon a smaller one at the side of the desk.

Jones sat down and continued fishing out papers. Nearly every sheet was covered with weird and extraordinary-looking diagrams, consisting of conic sections, parabolas, tangents, segments of circles that began in space and ended in a wilderness inhabited by lost letters of the alphabet which seemed to be hitched to numbers like draught horses.

'I have made no special calculations since the murder,' said Jones presently, glancing up at Clay. 'But — I am speaking now simply from the evidence of mathematics — there appears grave doubts as to Vintner's guilt.'

'Why?' grunted Clay.

'Because this murder contains an unexpected element, something of mixed passions probably more complicated than either robbery or revenge — or both.'

'What about Jenny?'

'I can't answer you yet.'

'Suppose Vintner broke in to rob the safe, found Mr. Embrich there, and stabbed him to save himself. You say those motives ain't mixed enough?'

'That would eliminate Mr. Goodloe as an accessory, Mr. Clay,' interposed Rosanna calmly.

Clay snorted, and Jones noticed that he no longer tried to placate the girl as before. 'Oh, well, we're just supposin', now,' he answered. 'How about that, Mr. Jones?'

'I say it would be impossible, because no murder of that character can take place in this part of Manhattan until the third week in April, unless we assume a combination of highly unlikely coincidences into which it would be absurd to enter.'

'Does this system of yours prophesy as well as — as find out things?' asked Clay with heavy sarcasm which was entirely lost on Jones, who was warming to authority rapidly.

'It does,' he answered enthusiastically, rubbing his hands together. 'Time does not exist so far as the laws of probability are concerned. And it enables me to say with conviction that the murder of Cyrus K. Embrich was due to obscure and unusual motives.'

Clay flicked the ash from his cigar. 'How do you dope all that out?' he asked.

'I'll try to make it clear to you, Inspector. We know that every event within the social system has a certain periodicity. For example, you don't have seven homicides in New York one year and three hundred the next.'

'Thank God for that!' said Clay heartily. 'Well, I think I get you there, Mr. Jones. You mean, statistics show that everything happens once every so often, taken by and large.'

'Precisely. And the longer the period covered in our investigations, the closer the approximation. Therefore, if we make our period infinity, our conclusions are absolutely correct. For example, there may be five times as many murders one week as the next, but hardly one month as the next, and never, by any chance, one year as the next.'

'Accordin' to that,' said Clay, 'there's almost exactly as many murders one century as in the next century.'

'Now that,' said Jones, 'is exactly where probability comes in. New York probably showed several thousand times as many murders in the nineteenth century as in the eighteenth. Why? Because of the introduction of certain factors which we term 'variables.' For instance, the city grew by leaps and bounds, changed from a provincial town to a metropolis, altered in social and racial composition; other variables are the perfection of the revolver and automatic pistol, the aggregation of great wealth in definite regions, etcetera. We see, then, that we are really dealing with a form of indeterminate equation to which there may be a dozen answers.

'Now, the number of murders in any

arbitrarily selected district of New York will be approximately the same year by year, subject to the same conditions — not exactly the same, but varying surprisingly little, and always within certain definite limits. You will also find that, whenever the murder rate shows a perceptible increase or decrease, certain 'variables' will also vary in exact proportion.'

Jones pulled out a square of paper covered with a network of curved lines and tangents skirting blotchy parabolas. Dotted about on it were letters and algebraic symbols. 'This line,' said Jones, 'represents that expectation of murders in downtown Manhattan west of Park Row during the twelve months ending June the first. You will see that thirteen of these have already been fulfilled. The thirteenth was that of Mr. Embrich.

'Nine were murders of passion and jealousy, of which eight occurred in the Italian quarter and one in the Syrian. Three were tong feuds in Chinatown. One of those still to come will be committed in the course of a hold-up,

129

two more will contain the love element, and one will be of revenge. One — Mr. Embrich's — was due to some unusual motive at present unknown to us.'

'And how do you know that Mr. Embrich's murder wasn't the one caused by revenge?' asked Clay.

'Because,' Jones answered, 'the murders having revenge as their motive have exceeded their average for many months past, always due to an ascertained decrease in other computed variables, and the series cannot continue on account of other factors having come to an end. On the other hand, for the past eleven and a half weeks certain recurrent variables have been below par — saving up for something big, as you might say. It's like roulette. When red has turned up persistently for an hour, you know a run of black is bound to occur. You can't say when, because the laws of variables are obscure. But — ' He looked at Clay earnestly. ' — I claim you could say *when*, to the very throw of the ball and spin of the wheel, if it were possible to collage these variables and have them ready at the precise moment.'

Clay remained silent. He had hardly the slightest notion what Jones was driving at. Practical experience told him that the mathematician scored successes where the utmost efforts of the city's detective force had failed. Dogged, unyielding, he was compelled, nevertheless, to recognize that fact. Still, in his mind, Clay ascribed Jones's success to luck. Possessing a rudimentary knowledge of psychology, he considered, furthermore, that Jones had powers of subconscious observation which shaped his deductions unconsciously.

So he sat staring at the diagram, which rapidly obscured itself into incomprehensibility before his eyes. 'Mr. Jones,' he said, 'if it wasn't you, and if you hadn't done the things I know you've done, I'd say that the man who handed me that line of talk was plumb crazy. You mean to tell me that Mr. Embrich's murder was just *bound to happen?* Couldn't have been stopped?'

'A murder of this *character* was bound to happen,' answered Jones. 'Mr. Embrich himself lies outside the scope of my calculations. I cannot estimate the innumerable variables attending upon the life of any man.'

'Well, Mr. Jones,' said Clay, 'all I can say is you've got me going. What you say sounds to me like Lumpkin killin' Mr. Embrich over those fried potatoes. And then there's another thing still got me stumped.' He rested his thick hands upon his knee and looked steadily at Rosanna, who returned his gaze without flinching. 'How did you know about that handkerchief, Miss Beach, seein' you were not in the room when I was questionin' Jenny?' he asked the girl. 'I guessed from the way you spoke to me that Mr. Jones hadn't then mentioned that fact to you. If I'm wrong, set me right, and we'll agree there's nothin' queer about it at all. And, in particular, I'd like to know how you guessed that that handkerchief was an embroidered one.'

Rosanna's eyes fell. She moved her hands nervously. 'Mr. Clay, I — I *can* tell you,' she answered, in low, almost faltering tones.

'Meanin',' said Clay, 'that you prefer

not to? Mr. Jones hadn't happened to mention about it to you when you asked me, then?'

'No,' answered Rosanna, in the same low tone.

Jones intervened. 'Miss Beach doesn't mean that she won't tell you, but that she can't,' he explained. 'It's quite correct that she inferred the existence of that handkerchief without my having said a word to her about it, and it struck me as one of the most extraordinary things I'd ever heard of. I tried to get it out of her how she did it, and she doesn't seem able to explain the matter at all.'

'*Humph!*' grunted Clay, turning a sharp look upon each of them alternately.

'The fact is,' Jones went on enthusiastically, 'this little girl's a natural-born detective. I don't believe that she had any idea of her powers when she first came to me as my stenographer, but I've been finding them out amazingly ever since. This isn't the first time, either. You remember what a help she was to me when we were after Vintner before. She's got uncanny powers of observation and deduction, which simply stagger me. But she doesn't know how she uses them.'

'That's all right,' answered Clay. 'She might have guessed that the floor'd been scrubbed with a handkerchief. But that don't explain the embroidered part of the business. And what do you mean by *'doesn't know how she uses 'em'?'*'

'I mean,' Jones answered, 'that the processes of deduction and inference are carried out in the unconscious part of her mind. It's like calculating geniuses who can immediately give you the cube root of the longest string of figures that you can think of, without having the slightest idea how they do it. Miss Beach simply doesn't know how she inferred the existence of that handkerchief.'

'Humph!' grunted Clay again, and turned his sardonic, searching gaze upon Rosanna, who, as if compelled by it, slowly raised her head and looked him in the face. 'Mighty useful power, I must say! We need it in my department — badly.' He turned to Rosanna. 'Now, about Mr. Goodloe,' he said. 'Ya know, we're still holding Vintner on that charge

of havin' burglars' tools, until we get somethin' more to go on. Well, Mr. Goodloe won't have to kick his heels in suspense much longer. There'll be somethin' doin' in a shorter time than anyone guesses, and then, if he's innocent, as he says he is — why, he'll go free, of course.'

He stood up, the embodiment of self-satisfaction. 'So don't you worry, Miss Beach,' he concluded. 'And don't forget to call on us, Mr. Jones, if there's anything more you want. I only wish I could figure it out your way, instead of havin' to chase meself all over town.'

He went out with a nod. Jones and Rosanna looked at each other silently until the sound of his heavy footsteps had died away on the stairs. Then Rosanna left her chair and went and stood beside Jones, her hands clasped in front of her. 'I — I want — ' she began in a trembling voice, and then burst into helpless tears. She swayed and, as Jones was about to catch her, groped for the arm of the chair and sank into it.

She leaned back, her eyes half closed. Jones, quite helpless in the presence of a woman in distress, felt a wild impulse to put his arms about Rosanna and comfort her, and to defy the immutable laws of probability and ask Rosanna to be his wife, on the slim seven-percent chance of the third time of asking. It was not his mathematics but his decent instincts that held him from plunging against the inevitable. He had committed himself to the freeing of Goodloe, for Rosanna's sake, because she loved him.

Rosanna opened her eyes, sat up, and sighed. She patted her hair. 'Mr. Jones, I don't know what you're going to think of me if I go on in this way,' she said. 'You've been so fine all through, and so patient. You haven't even asked me what line I'm following. I believe that those repeated burglaries at Miss Orr's apartment may have some bearing on this case. Clay's not going to strike up a side-trail when he has his own theory cut and dried, of course. And, to do him justice, he thinks he's on the main road. Will you trust to my intuition in this one matter?' pleaded the girl. 'Won't you put this work aside, just for the day? I want you to accompany me to Miss Orr's apartment — I *should* call her Mrs. Embrich, I suppose. Here's her address.'

To Jones, the repeated burglaries seemed to him to have no conceivable bearing upon the matter. But smothering a sigh, Jones put on his hat.

8

They had a hasty lunch and then proceeded uptown, getting off at Madison Square and walking a short distance to the apartment which Mrs. Embrich had given as her address. It was a cheap, but not squalid building. The apartment was on the top story. Climbing the stairs, they stopped panting outside their goal.

It was some time after they had rung when she came to the door. She was in a negligee, her hair was tumbling about her shoulders, and her eyes were red. 'I suppose you're from headquarters, too,' she said wearily to Jones. 'Come inside.'

The apartment, which appeared to consist of two rooms and a bath, was very small. It was plainly furnished with the stock furniture supplied in apartments let ready for use, but a number of articles in the shape of cushions, small rugs, pictures and photographs showed the personality of the occupant. Over the mantel in the small living-room was a large photograph of Mr. Embrich.

'We're sorry to intrude — ' Jones began.

She cut him short. 'It's no intrusion,' she interrupted. 'I thought I'd satisfied you people with that certificate, but if there's any more questions, ask them. It's my dearest wish to do all that I can to bring the murderer of my husband to justice.'

'I might say, though,' said Jones, 'we are not *exactly* from headquarters, though we've been collaborating with them. I'm a private investigator — my name is Jones — and I've been called into this case by the expressed wish of Mr. Embrich before he died, in case anything happened.'

'He — he *expected* — what happened, then?' gasped the girl.

'I'm afraid it looks like it. We thought the man he feared was a discharged employee who has been arrested, but his guilt now looks quite problematical. I helped Mr. Embrich in a case once before. This lady — '

'Is 'Sannie' Beach!' exclaimed Mrs.

Embrich. 'My dear, I know you from my husband's description. And didn't I see you at the funeral? Dear Cyrus and I have talked about you for hours. He was so anxious about you, and so hopeful that you'd come back to live with him — and like me.'

'Mr. Jones and I were actually in the room when you first came to see Inspector Clay,' Rosanna said gently. 'I guess you didn't notice us before you fainted.'

Mrs. Embrich broke down. Rosanna's arms went about her, and the two women embraced in one of those outbursts of feminine friendship.

'I did so want you to come to like me, and so did dear Cyrus. And it was to have been announced in a few days' time. I was under contract with my theatrical producer — touring in New England — and couldn't break it, and didn't want to. So that was why we kept the news of the engagement secret.

'Some people thought I'd made a good catch, and was marrying your uncle, as I know you called him, just because he was a rich man, but that wasn't true at all. We cared for each other from the very beginning, and we were very happy, although he was so much older than me.

'Then headquarters has been worrying me. I've had three telephone calls, and a man named Myers has been to see me twice and asked all manner of impertinent questions. And when he suggested that I had forged my marriage certificate — '

'How contemptible!' exclaimed Rosanna.

'You do believe I'm — I'm a real person and not an impostor, Sannie? Oh, I'm so glad.'

Another spell of feminine embracing followed.

'Well, when he suggested *that*, it simply froze me,' Mrs. Embrich continued, 'so that for the life of me I couldn't tell him anything. Not that there was much to tell. But I'll be most glad to help you in any possible way, Mr. Jones,' she continued.

Nevertheless, it was Rosanna who asked, 'Have you any idea who it can have been? Had Uncle Cyrus any enemies that you know of?'

'Yes — one,' answered Mrs. Embrich. 'A bitter enemy. But I have no reason to suppose that he was the murderer of my poor husband, and I can't, in decency, give you his name unless I have that reason.'

Jones intervened. 'Mrs. Embrich, I really think that you ought to give us his name in confidence, so that we can at least investigate the matter. Please remember that we do not represent the police — I am simply a private agent, called in at the wish of your husband. You can be positively assured that the name will go no further unless your husband's death should prove to be closely linked up with this man's actions.'

'And then,' said Rosanna, 'it may afford us a clue.'

'You have no clue, then?'

'There was the ex-employee of whom Mr. Jones was speaking,' answered Rosanna. 'He has been arrested, as you must know — '

'My dear, nothing on earth would induce me to *look* at a newspaper,' she proclaimed emphatically.

'Well, he has been arrested, together with the girl he was going with — Jenny Friend.'

'Jenny Friend! Why, how absurd! My husband often spoke of her to me, though I have never seen her. Did you know that he helped her mother for nearly a year, when the family was in dire straits? That was just like Cyrus. *Jenny*! As well say it was *me*!'

'Then,' said Rosanna, 'possibly you don't know that the police have arrested Philip Goodloe.'

'No, indeed, I didn't know, but I see this is getting more and more absurd. Phil Goodloe, from what my husband has said about him, isn't man enough to murder a chicken. Cyrus used to ridicule him — oh, Sannie, dear, I forgot. I have put my foot into it now, haven't I? I'm so sorry,' she said in penitential confusion.

'Never mind, dear. We can't help our opinions,' answered Rosanna. 'But I'm sorry Uncle Cy made fun of Philip. And I know how fond he was of him, too. But Uncle Cy did think he was a little of a — a milksop, and forgot how delicate he was. He'd always been brought up to take care of himself. So you knew — ?'

'That you and Phil were engaged? Yes,

my husband told me there was a sort of engagement. You know, after he married me, he didn't care very much — he'd have been so glad to have you home again. And I rather gathered that it was more the idea of perpetuating the old partnership than any desire to bring you two together that made him so anxious about the marriage. It must be a terrible strain to you, to have Phil arrested,' she continued. 'But I know he's innocent, and you know it, and truth *will* come out.'

'That's what we're going to see,' said Rosanna earnestly. 'And I know you'll help us with all the means in your power.'

'Indeed I will,' answered Mrs. Embrich. 'Well, then, Mr. Jones, I'll give you this man's name. It's Sanford Rogers.'

Rosanna shook her head. 'That's a new one on me, dear,' she said. 'I never heard of him, and I thought I knew most of poor Uncle Cy's friends.'

She took Rosanna's hands in hers. 'Now listen, and be prepared for a mild shock,' she said. 'I'm going to let you into a secret. First, let me ask you this: Did your uncle belong to any societies?'

'Yes, he was a strong Freemason,' said Rosanna. 'And then he was — let me see! — he was an Elk, and an Ancient Buffalo, and a member of the Wholesalers' Fraternal Order, and of the Antiquarian Society of New York, and one or two other things. I used to try to persuade him not to let them make so many demands upon his time, but he was so enthusiastic.'

'My dear,' said Mrs. Embrich, smiling a little, 'your uncle was *never* admitted to the Freemasons' Order at all, nor to the Elks, nor the Buffaloes — nor to any of the others. Dear Cyrus — I'm sure I'm not doing him any injustice, nor betraying any confidences — was rather fond of gay times when he was young, and his liking for them didn't decrease any as he grew older. When you thought he was at the Elks and the Buffaloes and the Antiquarian Society, he was probably entertaining a bunch of men and girls at some gay little supper party.'

'*Oh!*' gasped Rosanna.

'But he was the nicest gentleman who ever lived. He wasn't a roué, or anything bad. He just liked a little fun, and to spend his money helping some of the girls who were having a hard time. I know it was all done innocently. Lots of people didn't believe that, and lots more couldn't, but I knew him, and I assure you it was so.' She spoke with strong emphasis, and continued: 'He often told me that he didn't want you ever to dream that he went into rather a mixed set. He respected you almost to the verge of fear. He thought you were strait-laced, and he was morbidly anxious to do his duty to your father. And he was dreadfully afraid of that secretary of his, Miss Martin. He said she was always trying to poke her nose into his affairs.'

'Dear Uncle Cy!' murmured Rosanna. 'How foolish of him! As if I should have cared!'

'Well, Mr. Rogers had taken me out to dine on the night that I met Cyrus,' she continued. 'I had never much cared for Mr. Rogers, but he seemed persistent and I was unable to get rid of him. But after I met your uncle it was rather a rapid case. It began on my part with admiration for him, when I found out some of the things that he had done for people. It ended with real love. He was such a dear — so worldly, and yet so . . . so unspotted by the world.

'Well, Mr. Rogers knew, of course, that I was fond of Mr. Embrich, though he never knew that we were married. And that was what was so horrid, my not being able to tell him and send him away. He was here only Tuesday evening, the janitor told me, and left a box of flowers for me. I wouldn't even open the box this morning, and I told the janitor to take it away. I'm glad I was out when he called. But, I haven't the least reason to suppose that Mr. Rogers was responsible for my husband's death, and I'm not going to be unfair, though goodness knows he hated him.'

'Do you think this Sanford Rogers hated my uncle enough to have been capable of murdering him?' asked Rosanna.

Adelaide's eyes filled. 'I — *I don't know*,' she answered. 'He was jealous of him, and he knew we cared for each other. I don't think it was that he loved me so much, but that he couldn't bear to be thwarted by having another man cut in. He used to abuse your uncle sometimes to me. But I won't say he hated him enough to murder him.'

'What sort of a man is this Sanford Rogers?' Jones inquired.

'He's a horrid, bald, middle-aged man with a nasty mustache — the sort that gets in the soup, you know. He always gave me the impression of having a cross, nagging wife and a large family in Newark, or Jamaica, or some other suburban place. At any rate he never spoke of marriage to me, but he was always hinting at eloping and that sort of thing in the half-joking way that a decent woman detests so much. He isn't a nice man at all, in the way Mr. Embrich was, and he hit up the pace with a lot of chorus girls before he knew me, and probably since. Mr. Embrich knew him in some sort of business way, I believe. I told him once that Mr. Rogers had abused him, but he wouldn't say a word against him; he just laughed.'

'Where can one find him if necessary?' asked Jones.

She shook her head. 'That,' she

answered, 'is supposed to be the one thing that no woman could extract from him. He always poses as a man of mystery — the horrid, vulgar creature! *Ugh!'*

'Adelaide,' said Rosanna, 'you'll see him again, won't you? You must, for dear Uncle Cy's sake. And you must do everything in your power to find out who he is and where he lives, even if you have to — to lead him on a little.'

'Trust me, if Sanford Rogers had a hand in *my* husband's murder, I'm going to lay him by the heels. And, till I'm sure one way or the other, I'm going to stick to him tighter than a leech.'

And she looked as if she meant it.

'But now,' said Rosanna, 'I'll tell you the principal thing Mr. Jones and I came to see you about tonight. What was it that you were telling Inspector Clay about some mysterious burglaries in your apartment?'

'Oh, that's terrible!' exclaimed Adelaide. 'I don't know in the least what to make of them. This is the third time that it's happened to me. It happened Tuesday night, before I got home — I found my apartment looking like a bargain counter after a sale. Everything was out of place. No ordinary burglar would have taken the time. It's much more like the work of some practical joker — only I don't know anybody who has any grudge against me, or who would have done such a thing in fun. I left my *last* apartment because of it. It happened twice there at intervals of a few weeks. It's always the same thing: somebody gets into my apartment and goes through everything with a fine-tooth comb — clothes, books, letters, everything I own.'

'And takes nothing?' asked Rosanna.

'Nothing at all. That's what makes it so queer. Yet my clothes and papers are left strewn all over the place and every pocket and reticule is turned inside out.'

'And you don't suspect this Sanford Rogers?'

'I'm positive it can't be him,' answered Adelaide, 'because the second time it happened he was on a business trip to the same town I happened to be playing. He telephoned me, asking if he could come and see me. Besides, what object could

Mr. Rogers possibly have?'

'The reason why I suggested Sanford Rogers,' said Jones, 'was that I thought he might possibly have been trying to find out whether you and Mr. Embrich were married.'

'I'm sure he never suspected that we were married. And then, you see, we were not married the first two times this burglary happened; those were some months ago, when my poor husband and I were hardly anything more than acquaintances. My moving to this apartment seems to have thrown my persecutor off the scent for a time.'

Rosanna got up. 'My dear, we're going to run that fox to earth,' she said. 'Trust Mr. Jones! I haven't worked with him for nothing. And you'll follow up that matter of Mr. Rogers, and let us know just as soon as anything happens. You'll find us in the telephone book — Mr. Jones, at any rate. His name's Aloysius Arthur.'

'You'll never find me without Miss Beach, as long as I can keep her,' said Jones, blushing at the revelation of his name.

Adelaide looked from one to the other with a quizzical smile. Rosanna, catching her glance, blushed almost as red as Jones.

Jones followed Rosanna out of the apartment, wondering if the person who broke into Mrs. Embrich's apartment was the one who had murdered Cyrus Embrich. The 'strange and unusual' features of the affair, which the diagrams had prognosticated, would be fulfilled.

He was so absorbed in this speculation that he failed to see that his companion had stopped in the entrance, and he nearly knocked her over. Rosanna was standing with one fingertip pressed against the janitor's bell. 'Mr. Jones, I want you to interrogate whoever is in charge of this place,' she said as she rang. 'Find out all the particulars that you can about the burglary, and about Sanford Rogers. It's the burglary, remember; don't ask anything about the murder, or about Uncle Cy. I expect they don't know yet that Adelaide was *married* to him.'

Jones had time to grasp the implications of Rosanna's suggestion and to nod back before the janitor, a frowsy-looking man in a collarless shirt with a stiff, dented and very dirty starched front, came up the steps.

'You're the janitor?' asked Jones.

'Well, whadjerwant?' he snarled.

'I'm with headquarters,' said Jones, 'and I want to have a little talk with you about that burglary in Miss Orr's apartment. So, friend, loosen up and tell all you know about it.'

'I don't know nothin' about it,' answered the man sullenly. 'I ain't to blame if anyone gets up them stairs. The front door's supposed to lock, and it don't, and I've spoke to the landlord twice about it already.'

'This burglary took place on Tuesday night, I understand,' said Jones. 'Did you see the man?'

'*Nah!* Wouldn't I have held him if I had? I tell you I don't know nothin' about it.'

'How long had Miss Orr been out of town?'

'She come back night before last, late — '

'I know that. How long was she away?'

'Two or three weeks, maybe. Say, if you think — '

'If I *thought* what you *think* I'm *thinking*,' said Jones with emphasis, 'I wouldn't be talking to you *here*, but in the station-house. Get *that* straight, *friend*.'

The man's demeanor changed at once. 'I'll answer anything you want to know,' he muttered, 'only, I ain't to blame, as I said before. The door don't lock — you just go up and try it for yourself. I cleaned up her apartment after supper, and she hadn't come back then.'

'So you *clean* Miss Orr's apartment? How often?'

'Once a week when she's away. She leaves the key with me. That shows she don't think I go through her things. And I take her mail up to her room when there's anything too big to go into the letter-box.'

'When did you discover that someone had been in Miss Orr's apartment?'

'Wednesday evening. The place looked as if a mad bull'd been through it. But I didn't know it was a burglar.'

154

'And when were you in the apartment before that?'

'The afternoon before. A gent came with a box of flowers, and when she didn't answer he rang my bell. I took the box up, and the place was as clean as a whistle then.'

'What time did Sanford Rogers bring that box of flowers?'

The mention of Rogers's name appeared to impress the janitor, whose tone had a perceptibly cringing note as he answered, 'Between five and six o'clock, I should say. It was a big, long box. I took it straight upstairs.'

'Mr. Rogers asked for Miss Orr?'

'He did, and I told him she was out of town, and I didn't know how long it'd be before she came back. He looked sorry to hear it.'

'He's been coming here to see Miss Orr a good deal, hasn't he?'

'Not as often as he used to, before Miss Orr's new friend started visiting her — an old gent with a gray beard. I don't know who he is. Of course, I don't see the people who call more'n one time out of

155

fifty, but I know he used to come, three or four times a week regular — Mr. Rogers, I mean — before the new guy started visiting her.'

There was no indication of guile in the janitor's remarks. It was quite probable that the man did not know Adelaide Orr's visitor had been Cyrus Embrich, or that he had been her husband.

'When did you speak to Miss Orr about the flowers and the burglary?' asked Jones.

'I put the box on her table. There wasn't no need to tell her who'd brought them. There was his name on the card, tucked under the string of the box. She couldn't help seeing it. Nor there wasn't no need to tell Miss Orr that someone had been in her rooms. She could see that as soon as she went in.'

'When did you see Miss Orr?'

'Why, she came down here yesterday morning at about nine. She was sort of hysterical about who'd been in her room, and kept questioning me if I hadn't seen nobody. Then she said she was going for the police. She seemed half dippy, and she threw the box on my table, and said she didn't care what was in it, and I wasn't never to let Mr. Rogers in no more, if ever he rung my bell again. That's all I got to say, and I'm ready to swear to it, and if you think I had any hand in that job — well, you've got another guess coming.'

'What did you do with the box?' asked Jones.

He was not aware that Rosanna was no longer by his side until her voice answered his question out of the darkness. She was coming toward him, and in her hand she held an oblong box of cardboard. She carried it into the room. 'Here it is,' said Rosanna. 'I found it in the garbage can.'

'*See here!*' shouted the janitor in sudden anger.

But neither Jones nor Rosanna was more than partly conscious of the man's outburst. They were staring at the box. It had no label, the lid was broken, and most of the contents had been thrown away; in the bottom were two white, wilted lilies!

9

Jones and Rosanna turned and looked at each other. Jones's momentary feeling was one of consternation and bewilderment. Whenever he was up against a solid clue like this one, his mind groped helplessly, and he had an almost irresistible impulse to fly to some mathematical shelter.

The two left the apartment and walked quickly westward to Madison Square. They entered the park, and Rosanna seated herself upon a bench, making room for Jones beside her. She held out a soiled piece of pasteboard. 'Exhibit One,' she said.

On it Jones read, 'Mr. Sanford Rogers.' There was no address, but in one corner of the card was penciled: 'With fondest remembrances and regrets.'

'Mr. Jones,' said Rosanna, 'I've seen that writing before. I know I have — and I can't remember where. But I feel as if

I'm just on the point of remembering. I seem to know it well.'

'Was it written by some acquaintance of your uncle's, do you suppose?' Jones prompted.

She shook her head in doubt. 'I don't know. It seems as I know it almost as well as I know my uncle's hand.' She thought for some time, and then shook her head despondently. 'I can't place it,' she said. 'But here's Exhibit Two — the florist's label. It was pasted lightly on the box and seems to have come off naturally. No mystery about that.' She handed him a soiled slip, with the name and address of a Broadway florist on it.

Jones whistled. He looked at her exultantly. 'We've got him now,' he said.

'How?' asked Rosanna.

'Why, you know the class Larrabee caters to. He's right in the heart of the Tenderloin district. If this Sanford Rogers is the sort of gay boy Mrs. Embrich thinks he is, he must be well known at Larrabee's.'

'I should say,' answered Rosanna, 'that Mr. Sanford Rogers is probably clever enough to cover up his tracks, especially if he has a wife and a large family. But anyway, I'd be willing to wager we couldn't get his address at Larrabee's, even if they knew it. Larrabee's are too wise for that. However — ' She broke off to stare at a freckle-faced boy with flaming red hair who came whistling along the street that bordered the south side of the Square. Rosanna went toward him and beckoned. The boy, swinging smartly upon his heel, came toward her, grinning all over his features.

'What are you doing up this way?' said Rosanna.

The boy grinned noncommittally, and vouchsafed no answer. Rosanna continued: 'I guess you're doing a little private investigating of your own, maybe?'

The boy snorted. 'Well, I guess I *have*, miss!' he answered. 'Say, I followed a guy the whole day once, from nine o'clock one mornin' till two o'clock the next! Jest picked him up as he was comin' out of his house. Gee, he led me a dance before I saw him home to bed. Took me to some snide joints, too!'

'And he never knew he was being followed?' asked Rosanna.

'Never got wise! Say, he kep' me waitin' three hours outside his office, runnin' up and down the stairs so as the elevator fellers shouldn't spot me being on the job, and then he called on a girl for three hours more in the afternoon, and wound up hittin' the white lights. Now, wouldn't that jar you?'

'You certainly stuck to it,' said Rosanna. 'You like trailing people, then?'

'Like it? Say, if I hadn't me papers to sell — '

'Suppose I gave you a little job to try out for me,' Rosanna suggested.

'*You?* Why, you ain't married, miss, are you? Say, if you are, jest show me the feller, and I'll turn in me report complete tomorrow!'

Rosanna laughed merrily. 'No, I'm not married, Bobby,' she answered. 'It's something quite different. Know Larrabee's, the florist's?'

The boy nodded, fixing his bright eyes keenly upon her face.

'Well, there's a gentleman who buys

161

flowers there sometimes, and we want to find out where he lives. He's a bald, middle-aged man with a nasty mustache — you know the kind.'

'Never saw one I liked,' said Bobby.

'So you won't find it very difficult to spot him. Do you think, after you've sold your papers downtown, you could take up your stand outside Larrabee's, around five, and sell some more, and keep a sharp lookout for this gentleman? He may be in there any evening around that time.'

'Sure! That ain't hard.'

'Then follow him! If he goes into a house or apartment, look at the name over the button he pushes, and make sure he isn't visiting instead of going home. If it's an elevator apartment, just use your judgment. You'll know what to do, if you have the makings of a detective in you.'

The boy grinned. 'You jest trust me, miss!' he answered. 'I'll get him for you!'

'And when you're sure you've found his home, report to this gentleman here.'

'Where'll I find him?' asked the boy, casting a supercilious glance at Jones.

Jones thought for a moment. 'Suppose

I come here every evening at seven,' he suggested. 'It's not far from where I board. I could take a stroll this way, and if this boy has found out anything, he can be here.'

'I get you,' said Bobby laconically. 'Good evening, miss.' And, with a touch of the cap, and something of a grand gesture, he started up the street, walking with all the dignity of a newly hatched chick, or, rather, perhaps, a real detective in the hatching.

'Who in the world is that?' asked Jones. 'You seemed to know him.'

'Oh, Mr. Jones,' Rosanna laughed, 'what a detective you make! That's Bobby Mann, and you were face to face with him for half an hour on Wednesday evening!'

'I thought I'd seen him before,' commented Jones.

'Now, Mr. Jones,' Rosanna said, 'I want you to come with me to my uncle's house. I feel, somehow, that if I were there — in the library — I'd remember about that writing. I'm so near knowing now, it's almost bursting in my brain.

Won't you come?'

During the ride uptown she did not utter a word, but remained with brows knit, staring at the floor. The gloomy Peck opened the door of the Embrich house to them. At the sight of them he gave a perceptible start, and looked at Rosanna in his furtive way.

'Good evening, Miss Beach,' he said. He stood blocking the entrance, regarding the girl with unmistakable insolence. He seemed to Jones to be making up his mind not to admit them. As Jones approached him, however, he drew back a step or two, and Jones, taking Rosanna by the arm, led her past him.

He accompanied her along the passage into the library at the rear. Rosanna snapped on the light. The room appeared to have been untouched since Embrich's death; dust had collected and lay white upon the surfaces of the furniture everywhere.

Rosanna shuddered. 'It seems impossible to realize he's not here,' she murmured. 'We used to sit here so much. Now . . . '

Peck had come shambling after them. 'Was there anything you *wanted*, Miss Beach?' he asked, standing in the doorway with a look of obstinate malevolence upon his furtive face. There was a subtle threat in his tone, under the respectfulness, as if Peck denied Rosanna's right to be there.

'Nothing at present, Peck,' Rosanna returned. 'I'll ring if I want anything.'

'Very good, Miss Beach,' said Peck, still waiting.

'Get out!' said Jones. 'And close that door!'

Peck withdrew slowly, and they heard the sound of his footsteps apparently retreating along the passage. Rosanna went softly to the door and locked it. Having done this, she stood still in the middle of the room, looking at Jones in perplexity. 'It was in *here* I saw that writing,' she said. 'My uncle used to write all his letters here. Perhaps — perhaps it was a letter from somebody. Oh, if only I could remember! I know it was here!'

She sat down in a chair, resting her chin on her hands, deep in thought.

Minutes went by. Jones began to grow uneasy. He could hear Peck shuffling somewhere near at hand. Once he thought there was a rustle outside the door, but he only sat watching Rosanna.

The girl got up slowly. 'It's no use,' she muttered, and walked to the bookshelves, which she scanned with a hopeless expression. Suddenly, with a little cry, she snatched at one of the books on the lower shelf. It was a child's storybook. She brought it to the table before the window and opened it to the fly-leaf.

'Look! I've got it!' she cried in exultation. 'Just instinct! It came to me when I stood there before the shelves. My uncle used to read it to me sometimes when I was a child. Look, Mr. Jones!' she cried, as she pointed to something written on the fly-leaf of the volume.

There was an inscription on the storybook in ink yellow with age, as follows:

'To Miss Rosanna, wishing her a happy birthday and many more of them, with remembrances from some employees of her father and Mr. Embrich.'

The girl laid the card down upon the leaf beneath the writing and looked at Jones. 'Compare them!' she said with suppressed eagerness. 'Don't you see the resemblance? They were written by the same man!'

'Why, it's the same writing — it certainly *is* the same!' exclaimed Jones in astonishment. 'And there's the identical word, 'remembrances,' without a change!'

Rosanna nodded. 'It's odd how that book suddenly flashed into my mind, and how I remembered that the writing was the same,' she said. 'It almost looks as if there may be something to that tale you told Clay in your office, about being a subconscious genius. I was only about nine when this book was given to me, and I haven't thought of it for years. Recall that Adelaide said she thought Mr. Sanford Rogers had a family in Newark or Jamaica? And recall how she described him?' Jones nodded. 'Actually, he lives in the Bronx, and he has a cross, horrid wife, and a large family.'

'Who lives in the Bronx?' demanded Jones.

'Why, Mr. Timson, Mr. Embrich's assistant manager.'

'*Timson?*' Jones shouted the name so loud in his excitement that Rosanna placed her finger emphatically on her lips and pointed toward the door.

'That inscription was written by Mr. Timson. Therefore Timson and Sanford Rogers are the same man.'

'Then everything is explained and we have the solution,' answered Jones. 'Adelaide Embrich has supplied the motive. Clay must be informed at once.'

'You think, then, that Mr. Timson is guilty of my uncle's murder?' asked Rosanna.

'Guilty? Of course he's *guilty*!' cried Jones, raising his voice again almost to a bellow. But Rosanna's next words came like a bucket of cold water.

'Do you think,' she asked, 'that Inspector Clay will arrest Mr. Timson on the strength of my statement that he wrote that inscription, and so break down his own theories? Besides,' she went on, remorselessly, 'what does this prove? The lilies were delivered at Adelaide's apartment several hours before my uncle's murder.

Is it reasonable that Mr. Timson kept back two of them with the express purpose of placing them on my uncle's desk after he had killed him? Why, everybody is giving lilies at this season! And how does this link Mr. Timson with the murder? What does it prove? It doesn't prove anything!'

'You believe, then, that Mr. Timson did not murder Mr. Embrich?' asked Jones.

'I believe whoever killed my uncle *also* breaks into Adelaide's apartment. I believe that the clue lies there. If Timson can be shown to be that man, then I'll believe that he's the murderer.'

Jones groaned. 'It's getting deeper and deeper,' he muttered. 'Honestly, Miss Beach, we'd simply be saving ourselves trouble if we sat down calmly and scientifically planned it out according to the immutable laws of mathematics. However, I suppose we'd better follow up this trail.'

'How?'

'Go to Timson's apartment.'

'You mean the one in the Bronx, or — ?'

'Or the one Bobby Mann's searching for? If we went to his home we'd only scare him away. But how about informing Clay?'

'I want — *listen*!' She held up a finger in swift warning, then crept noiselessly toward the door. The faint ring of a telephone came to their ears. The hum of indistinguishable words followed it. Finally came the click of the receiver being hung up in place.

Jones saw that Rosanna was trembling. 'I want to get out of this place at once!' she whispered weakly.

He flung the door open, to discover Peck tiptoeing noiselessly toward the library. At the sight of them the butler stopped and looked at them with a sneering smile. 'Mayn't I bring you a cup of tea, Miss Beach?' he asked.

'Nothing, Peck, thank you,' replied Rosanna.

But as she approached Peck stood still, filling the passage. Jones brushed past the girl and seized him by the lapels. 'See here, friend,' he said, 'I don't know what you mean by your insolence to Miss

170

Beach, but next time you feel like annoying her, or listening at doors, remember me. My name's Jones.' He shook the butler vigorously to and fro until his lank red hair, falling over his eyes, forced him to let him go.

Peck squirmed out of his grasp. He stood behind them in the passage, chattering, 'You'll pay for this assault, Jones or no Jones! I know my duties!'

Jones opened the door, took Rosanna by the arm, and led her down the steps. 'I'm going to call a taxi and take you home,' he said.

'No — to the office,' answered Rosanna faintly.

'The office — *tonight?* There's nothing to do *there* — at least, nothing that can't wait 'til tomorrow,' said Jones quickly.

'No, you *must* take me there!' exclaimed the girl in agitation. 'I — there's something that I must tell you. I can't tell you here — anywhere else.'

Jones accordingly called a taxi, in spite of Rosanna's protests. The door was closed, but Jones, who often worked late, had a key by arrangement with the owner and, having opened it, he helped Rosanna up the stairs and into the office.

'Now this was foolish!' said Jones, assuming an unwonted dictatorial attitude. 'Miss Beach, I believe this case has simply shattered your nerves, as it naturally would. I don't believe I ought to let you — '

'Oh, don't stand there chattering about what you believe!' cried the girl excitedly, reducing her companion to instant, surprised, submissive silence. 'Get me a glass of water, Mr. Jones, please!'

Jones took the tumbler and went along the passage to the tap. He had just filled it and was about to return when he heard a crash within his office. Running at full speed, and spilling nearly all the contents of the tumbler en route, he entered the room to find Rosanna lying unconscious upon the floor, her overturned chair beside her, and the two volumes of Boyle's *Inquiry Into the Laws of Averages* open, and now coverless, among the ruins.

He set the glass down, picked the girl up in his arms, and placed her in her chair. Rosanna stirred and sighed faintly.

There was a nasty cut on her forehead, from which a trickle of blood was oozing. Half-frantic, Jones waved his hands vigorously before the girl's face, tried to force sips of water between her lips, and as a last resort poured a little water into one palm and flicked it into her eyes, all the while beseeching her to come back to consciousness.

When, at length, Rosanna opened her eyes and waved one hand to signify to him to desist from these attentions, Jones began to look about him. He was not much better at inference than at observation, but the position of the chair and the sharp edge of the projecting lower portion of the bookcase told a plain story. Rosanna had fallen from her chair while endeavoring to reach the volumes.

Jones picked them up. The dark gap overhead was above his reach, and partly filled by the sideward collapse of adjacent volumes. So he threw them on the desk, where they sank into a couch of diagrams, emitting a dusty spray.

He knitted his brows in perplexity. It was on the Wednesday afternoon, upon returning from the store, that Rosanna had likewise sent him for a glass of water and, during his absence, made a similar attempt to reach Boyle. But he had then explained to her that Boyle's researches had been rendered obsolete by the researches of later statisticians.

He could not understand it, and, characteristically, he assumed that he had not made his point clear. So when Rosanna, after a few moments' rest, rose up from her chair, pale, but apparently composed again, he said:

'Miss Beach, about Boyle — er — I thought you understood that he was not much in use in computing variables. It's a rare old book, but rather unnecessarily drawn out. That *Theorem on Mortality*, which I suppose interested you particularly, has been rendered obsolete by the later actuaries' reports.'

Rosanna sighed, but did not interrupt. She had to let Jones finish. But her next speech was more directly to the point. 'Mr. Jones,' she said, 'I want you to understand — I'm leaving you tonight. I can't work here anymore.'

Jones stared at her in stupefaction. 'You're *leaving me*?' he gasped. 'Why, you — you *can't*, Miss Beach! It was all right before you came, when I hadn't tackled cases like this one, requiring personal investigation, but — ' He broke into an agitated stammer. 'See here, now, Miss Beach, I've been telling you all along you oughtn't to have come in on this job. Suppose you take a nice little holiday for two or three weeks at my expense! Salary to continue. And — I know you're not getting what you should, but I've been meaning to ask you if you wouldn't mind letting me — letting me raise your — '

'Oh, *do* be quiet,' exclaimed Rosanna. 'I don't want any holiday, and I don't want any raise of salary. I — just — can't stay. And I — just — can't — tell you — why.'

Jones looked at her in despair. 'Miss Beach,' he said mournfully, 'I'd do anything to keep you. And you did say that you wanted to stick, because it was your duty to Mr. Embrich to try to discover his murderer. However, I suppose there's nothing I can do to persuade you. Where shall

I send your check? I could make it out now, only I've mislaid my book.' He glanced despairingly at the mass of papers upon the desk. 'It's under there somewhere,' he said in lugubrious tones.

'Just keep it for me 'til you hear from me,' answered Rosanna. Then she took a step toward him and held out her hands impulsively. 'Oh, Mr. Jones, you won't misunderstand me, will you?' she said beseechingly. 'It isn't because I don't like the work, or you. I just must go. You'll understand my reason soon.'

Tears came into her eyes. 'Just try to trust me,' she continued. 'And, if you'll forgive me, I want to beg one thing of you. Don't tell Inspector Clay about our discovery. And follow your clue. It'll lead right. I know it will. It will lead to Philip's vindication, and — just trust me, will you? Promise?'

'Of course I promise,' answered Jones, feeling his heart racing madly.

A moment later he found himself alone, listening to the faint sound of the girl's footsteps on the stairs of the old building, with the knowledge that all his world was slipping away from him.

His brain was whirling as he began to pace the little office.

He stopped. He shook himself like a great tawny retriever dog. His eyes fell on the piles of papers littering his desk. 'Oh, shucks!' said Jones, seating himself in his swivel-chair.

And he plunged resolutely into his long-deferred work, sorting his sheets, crumpling discarded ones into balls and pitching them into corners of the room, until at last the Embrich diagram began to grow under his moving pen.

Circles clove circles; tangents, representing the eighty-five murder variables, radiated out of all corners of the compass and intersected segments; the alphabet ran riot among it all, and, as the diagram became more complex, Jones, forgetting all else, sat muttering and brooding over it, like a god presiding over a world.

Dawn crept into the room. The rumble of the traffic filled the streets. Jones sat unconscious of the flight of the hours. By eight o'clock he had laid aside his pen now and was staring at a series of values which summed up hours of mathematical work. He shook his tousled head. At last he pushed his chair back and was beginning to pace the room again when there came a tramp along the passage and a letter, thrust through the slit, dropped to the floor. He looked at it, recognized Rosanna's writing, and opened it. He read:

'I am sending you a few lines before I leave New York to remind you of what I asked you, and to assure you that I have not thrown up the case. I couldn't tell you in your office, but I can say now that I have left because I need to be alone in order to follow my own line of investigations. Believe me and trust me if you can.'

It was signed 'Rosanna.'

Jones laid the letter face upward upon his desk, and sat down in his chair again. Once more he plunged into his problem.

He was so absorbed in it that he was entirely unconscious of the heavier tramp along the corridor until the door opened.

Then he looked up into the sardonic, sneering, sinister face of Clay.

10

'Mornin',' said the inspector, nodding coolly at Jones. 'Early at work, I see.'

'I've been here all night,' answered Jones. 'I had to get this job finished. The worst of it is, it's almost impossible to leave off in the middle and take it up again.'

'Say, you certainly are some stayer, Mr. Jones!' said Clay in mock admiration. 'Partner not come down yet?'

Jones shook his head in mournful recollection of the events of the preceding evening. 'I'm afraid Miss Beach won't be here anymore,' he said.

'Not comin' anymore! How's that?' demanded the inspector sharply.

'She's left me,' answered Jones, swinging round in his chair. 'Told me only last night that she quit. I was astounded.'

Clay, letting one heavy eyelid flicker an instant on his cheek, answered, 'I sort of guessed she mightn't be here. So she flew

179

the coop last night, eh?' He nodded briskly, pursing his thick lips. 'That her swan song, Mr. Jones?'

Seeing Rosanna's signature to the letter lying on Jones's desk, Inspector Clay picked the missive up and read it. Jones's momentary indignation was smothered by the feeling of intense depression. He had not the heart to display resentment.

'What's the meanin' of this she says about your rememberin' what she asked you?' Clay inquired, laying the letter down.

'A matter of office routine,' answered Jones, beginning to take fire at Clay's cross-questioning, and yet held back by the dim forebodings of evil to come.

'You say you spent all last night dopin' out this mystery, Mr. Jones,' he said. 'Well, I'd sure be interested to know just what conclusions you've arrived at.'

Jones became all animation instantly. He pulled the chart toward him and took up his pen. 'Yes, all night,' he answered, 'and I've succeeded in bringing it down to a single indeterminate equation.' He pushed the diagram toward Inspector

Clay, who had perched himself upon the edge of the table, and was looking alternately from it to Jones, with a clearly puzzled expression upon his face.

'There,' said Jones solemnly, tapping the paper with his fingernail, 'there stands for me proof absolute of design in nature, proof of a living God! If any man dare say the universe is the result of the fortuitous concourse of flying atoms, I challenge him with that! Law, order — justice, Mr. Clay, lie proven on the surface of that single sheet!'

He looked up at the inspector, whose eyes, now fixed upon his own again, flashed a fierce challenge that Jones, filled with enthusiasm, failed utterly to see.

'No plainer or more irrefutable sign has ever been given to me,' said Jones. 'In fact, when I discovered it, it was like a blow in the face to me. This chart shows beyond question that a *woman* murdered Cyrus Embrich.'

'The *hell* you say!' said Clay.

'If not,' continued Jones, 'we have to face an impossible alternative requiring an entire shift of all the figures upon this diagram. This alternative, which I have not planned beyond the merest outlines, requires a holocaust, a convulsion of nature, and three railroad disasters on the same day.'

'I guess you won't need to examine into *that*, Mr. Jones,' said Clay sardonically. 'It looks much more like a woman murdered Mr. Embrich.'

'I'm glad that you agree with me,' said Jones enthusiastically. 'Of course, that is the correct alternative. But now I'm puzzled. You notice the presence of the shooting weapon — the second radius that falls within the small semicircle. There was a second person involved — a man, because this particular radius runs almost but not quite parallel to W, and yet cannot intersect it within the limits of the diagram.'

'The skirt had a sidekick with a gat,' translated Clay. 'Quite clear. Proceed!'

'Well,' said Jones, 'it appears that they were not in Mr. Embrich's office together at the time of the deed. In fact, I consider it doubtful whether they were as closely associated as one would naturally infer.

And that's what I'm worrying over.'

'Just how do ya mean?' demanded Clay.

'I should say that there was some discrepancy in their plans — they may even have planned the murder separately. You see, the line W — woman, remember — and the radius of the shooting implement diverge, instead of converge, when we trace them back to the murder circle. The curve of obscure motives I have not yet had time to trace. When I have done that, a great deal more will be revealed, and I hope enough to indicate with precision both the motives and the personality of the murderer.'

'No need to puzzle any more, Mr. Jones,' said Clay. 'Your system's a sure thing. I came to scoff, and you've got me at the mercy-seat. A man and woman did it, and that's enough for me. The man's name's Goodloe, and the girl's Rosanna Beach. And I've been wise to that from the beginnin'.'

For a single instant Jones sat as if petrified with horror. Then he leaped to his feet, doubling two huge fists, the while his features worked convulsively.

'You — *you damned dog!*' he bellowed.

Clay's self-control was marvelous; though his face had grown purple, and the points of his jaws stood out with the gritting of his teeth together, he answered in a perfectly smooth, even voice, 'Sit down, and listen to me, Jones, and I'll talk straight to you!'

For a moment Jones remained poised in his position, his taller but slighter figure towering over Clay. Then, with a deep groan, Jones sank into his chair and rested his chin in his hand.

Clay drew up a chair to his. 'You seen it comin'?' he asked, in tones almost of sympathy.

'I knew that Miss Beach was unduly worked up, even allowing for the fact that it was her adoptive father who had been murdered. Last night, when my investigations showed me beyond a doubt that a woman was principally concerned, I was staggered. I thought of Miss Martin, even of Mr. Embrich's wife. Both seemed impossible. But I never thought of Miss Beach for a single moment. Miss Beach?

Why, it's incredible. It's monstrous! Inspector Clay, I know that girl. I haven't had her working for me these many months for nothing. I tell you she went away because she sensed you suspected her. She told me another innocent person might be wrongly accused. The whole thing's clear now. She means to be free in order to run her uncle's murderer to earth.'

'You haven't convinced me on that point, Mr. Jones, but you've convinced me on another. I guess you do believe Miss Beach is innocent, and that you don't know where she's hidin'. When I came here I thought you did. I guessed you'd put that letter there to stall me. I believe now that you're simply the innocent bystander.

'However, I didn't come here to convince you against your will, Mr. Jones, nor yet in the hope of picking up Miss Beach. She'd flown the coop just about an hour when Myers got to her apartment. But we'll get her today, and I don't mind tellin' you there's been a spotter on this place since six o'clock this mornin'.

'But there's a little piece of evidence I'm looking for, and I'm looking for it *here*. I won't pretend I've got a search warrant, Mr. Jones, but I'm takin' you at your face value as the innocent bystander, and I guess you won't object. If you do — why, it won't make any difference, except that I'll have to hold you awhile.'

'Search me all you please, and be damned!' said Jones.

'Oh, it's not you, Mr. Jones,' responded the inspector suavely. 'It's your office. I don't know whether you'll remember how clumsy I was with a pail of water that mornin' we went down to have a look at the shippin' department. Miss Beach's rubbers left a pretty clear print on the floor afterward. I want those rubbers if they're here, Mr. Jones. Maybe they ain't, but I can survive the disappointment.'

'If Miss Beach left her rubbers here, they'll be under her desk,' Jones answered, glancing in that direction. 'As you see, they're not. If you think I'm hiding them, look anywhere you please.'

Clay, noting the gaping hole on the bookshelves, took Miss Beach's chair, and mounted it. 'Oh, I guess I won't need to do *that*, Mr. Jones,' he remarked suavely, plunging his arm into the gap left by the displaced Boyce. He drew his hand out. The fingers grasped a pair of woman's rubbers. On the soles were concentric rings. On Clay's face was the most sardonic smile that had ever rested there. He got down softly, replaced the chair in front of Rosanna's desk and, holding a rubber in either hand, stood watching Jones. 'Pretty strong, Mr. Jones,' he commented. 'But as I was sayin', I guess you didn't know.'

'I certainly did *not* know that Miss Beach kept her rubbers on the bookshelf,' answered Jones.

'You observed the pattern on the soles?' asked Clay, holding up the rubbers for closer inspection.

'You told me yourself that rubbers with that pattern are on sale at most of the stores.'

'I did. But what'd she want to hide 'em for?'

'I'll tell you why,' Jones answered, casting about desperately for some anchorage in the fog of his mind. 'She knew that you suspected her. And she wasn't going to have you run up a false trail when the capture of the murderer occupied all her thoughts. Maybe it wasn't well advised, but — that's why.'

Clay's smile began to broaden, and the sight of it infuriated the other.

'She's *innocent*,' cried Jones. 'I'll prove it — I *swear* I'll prove it!'

The inspector shrugged his shoulders. 'Meanwhile, suppose you let me do a little provin' myself,' he suggested. 'What I was goin' to remark was that I've an appointment with Vintner in about twenty minutes' time, and then I'm goin' to pay some other calls. If you think you can prove what you say you're goin' to prove, you might like to come along. Of course there's no compulsion, if you think you can do your provin' better sitting here and making circles.'

'I'll come,' said Jones. 'I'm here to look for the truth.'

'Which I think you'll find soon enough, Mr. Jones,' answered Clay significantly. 'Well, if you're ready . . . '

Jones clapped on his hat, and they left the office together. When they entered the outer office of the homicide bureau a little later, Vintner was already there. A young patrolman was also in the room.

Clay beckoned the whole lot into his office. 'Sit down, Mr. Jones. Mornin', Vintner. Think you've put one over on us, eh?'

Vintner gave an exhibition of his grin. 'Oh, I don't think nothin',' he answered, with a shrug of his shoulders.

Clay looked at the patrolman. 'Brannigan, have you ever see this man before?' he asked. Brannigan nodded. 'Well, when did you see him last?'

''twas in the Night Court on Tuesday evening. I never saw him before that night. I arrested him at the Central Park entrance, south side, at half past nine.'

'Go on!' barked Clay.

'I saw him standing with a woman at the south entrance at 9:15. I kept the pair under close observation, because they seemed to be having a disagreement about something. By the time I'd got near them they was both so worked up they didn't notice me. Then I heard him asking her to go with him again, and she refused, and called him a jail-bird. I was just going to have a look at him to see if I could identify him, when he hit her in the face. She started screaming, and they saw me at the same time, and made away in different directions. I couldn't take in both of 'em, and the woman hadn't done nothing, so I went after this man and got him before he'd gone more than fifty paces. I rapped, but you know it's a long beat, and by the time Flannery come up the woman had made her getaway. So I took this man to the station, and he was fined ten dollars in the Night Court.'

'What name did he give there?' asked the inspector.

'Name of Clay,' responded the patrolman, at which Vintner gave another grin.

'And you're sure this is the man?'

'Dead sure. I'd know him again in a hundred years by that smile of his,' responded the officer. 'Smiled all the time.'

'And you're prepared to testify on oath to what you're tellin' me?'

'I've done so, and I'm ready to do so again,' said Brannigan.

Clay drew in a long breath. 'If you were bein' fined in the Night Court at the time Mr. Embrich was bein' murdered, naturally you couldn't have been in Mr. Embrich's store at the same time,' he said to Vintner. 'But why in hell couldn't you have come through with that story when I saw you before?'

'Because I ain't doin' no talkin' till I seen my friends,' responded Vintner in a surly manner. 'You play and I follow. Get me?'

'All right, Bill. We'll play for the original charge, then,' answered Clay, who seemed in nowise disconcerted by Vintner's triumph.

When he had been taken back Clay asked Brannigan, 'Think you could identify the young woman? What sort of looker was she?'

'Pretty as a picture,' the patrolman answered. 'One of them natural blondes, with big baby eyes — blue I'd say, though I couldn't tell in the dark. He called her Jenny.'

'Now are you sure of that, or did you just read that was her name?' asked Clay.

'I'm dead sure,' said the policeman emphatically.

'You'd know her out of a dozen, would you?'

'Out of a hundred,' answered Brannigan.

'Well, I guess we won't put you to that trouble, but I'll take you to see her,' said the inspector.

Jones accompanied them to the Tombs. Jenny Friend was seated behind the bars of her cell in the women's part of the prison. When she looked up and recognized Clay the look of obstinacy came over her face again. She glanced quickly at Jones and the patrolman, but appeared not to know either of them.

'Well, Jenny,' said Clay, 'we're wise to you now.' He turned to the patrolman. 'This the woman?' he asked.

'That's her,' said Brannigan.

'You're sure, now? Remember, there's a good deal dependin' on what you say.'

'No doubt of it,' said Brannigan.

Clay dismissed him. As he turned to

Jenny again the girl broke out: 'Say, what're you trying to put over on me now? I've told you, as God's my witness — '

Clay raised a heavy hand. 'Can the chatter, Jenny!' he said. 'We're hep. Vintner's come through with it. We know now what you were doin' at half past nine on Tuesday evenin'.'

'I went for a walk, I tell you, and that's all you'll ever get out of me,' the girl persisted. 'Say, I'm not falling for any of that line of talk!'

Clay smiled. 'I'll tell you what you were doing, Jenny,' he said. 'You went for a walk with Vintner as far as Central Park. You had a few words there, and Vintner struck you in the face. We know all about it, Jenny.'

Jenny's nerve left her completely. She almost crumpled, and clutched at the bars for support. 'Oh, my Gawd!' she wailed. 'So you've got wise to it, have you?'

'Sure I have, and it's nothin' against you, Jenny,' said Clay cheerfully. 'What beats me is why you didn't come through with it before.'

'Come through? Who? *Me?*' cried Jenny. 'I'm a respectable girl, I am. To think that beast went back on me like that! That's the stuff you get handed, for being kind to a jail-bird!'

'How do you mean, 'being kind'?' asked Clay.

'Why, I used ter go with Vintner once, before I knew what sort of fellow he was, and when he was sent to the pen, naturally I gave him the mitt. Then, after he came out, he kept pesterin' me to go with him again, and he wouldn't let me alone. Well, I felt kinder sorry for him, because he was down and out, and at last I thought, if I was to meet him, I might be able to make him believe I'd meant what I said when I told him that there'd be nothing more doing between us. That's why I met him. I wasn't going to have it said as I was running round with a fellow just outer the pen.'

'Of course you weren't, Jenny,' said Clay, nodding his head encouragingly. 'And what happened when you met him?'

Jenny shrugged her shoulders. 'Why, he started asking me not to turn him down,' she said, 'and he kept telling me he'd got good money comin' in, and that I wouldn't have to work if I married him. I guessed what he meant, though he didn't say — '

'Didn't he tell you where it was comin' from?'

'No. He just kept talking, and I couldn't make him understand. He thought I was stallin' him. At last he woke up and asked me, short and nasty, if I was through with him. I told him I was, and then he — he *hit* me.'

'So that's why you wouldn't talk, eh?' asked Clay.

'Sure it was! I didn't think Vintner was cur enough to give me away, but I might have known a man who'd hit a lady wouldn't stick at that.'

Clay looked at her and appeared to reflect for a moment or two. 'Well,' he said at length, 'you've acted mighty foolish Jenny, and I guess you've more or less deserved what you've got. However, I believe you're tellin' me the truth now. But what more have you got to say about that handkerchief?'

'My Gawd, I keep telling you I've never *seen* it before!' exclaimed the girl. 'Don't I keep saying it's the initial of the *first name* that goes on handkerchiefs?'

'You do,' said Clay. 'However, I guess that's mostly a matter of individual taste. You haven't doped out any idea who it was put that handkerchief down the waste-pipe?'

Jenny shook her head vigorously. 'All my handkerchiefs are plain,' she said. 'Them with the initials are common. Ladies don't use 'em much. But I guess the person who stuffed it down there had got me in mind when it was done.'

Clay inclined his head. 'I'm beginnin' to think so too, Jenny,' he said. 'So I'm thinkin' of takin' a chance and lettin' you out of here.' He half-turned as if to go, then suddenly swung round upon his heel and asked, 'I suppose you don't happen to know who killed Mr. Embrich, do you, Jenny?'

'*Me?*' cried the girl, startled. 'For Gawd's sake, *no*!'

11

Jones followed the inspector out of the flagged corridor, but their immediate destination was not the street. He made his way toward the men's part of the prison, stopped, fumbled for his pass, and said, 'I guess what you've heard has about knocked out the idea of Jenny Friend and Vintner, Mr. Jones.'

'I never held it,' answered Jones.

'Well,' retorted Clay, 'you said it was a woman, with a man helpin' her in an indirect sort of way, and I'm goin' to pin you down there. We're goin' to see Mr. Goodloe. He was goin' to talk to me today. Got somethin' or other on his chest he's anxious to get rid of,' said Clay sardonically.

Goodloe's appearance was very different from Jenny's. He rose nervously from his seat, and when he came forward Jones could see that he seemed to have gone to pieces during his few days' incarceration. His cheeks, unshaven since the day before, had fallen in, his tie sagged beneath his crumpled collar, and he looked almost a nervous wreck.

'Mornin', Mr. Goodloe,' said Clay. 'This is Mr. Jones; you met in the office Wednesday. We're on the case together, and anything you want to say to me won't go any further than Mr. Jones, neither.'

Goodloe looked nervously from Clay to Jones and back again. His truculent, defiant manner had entirely disappeared. His attitude and his voice were almost cringing. He answered wearily, 'I guess it'd be best to speak frankly. I was a good deal startled when you found those fingerprints on the envelope-opener, and my first thought was to save others who might be implicated — unjustly, of course.'

'Quite so,' returned Clay sagely. 'Seems to me it'd be best to tell exactly what happened on Tuesday night, so far as is known to you. You've seen the first edition of the afternoon papers, no doubt. No? I'm surprised, sir.'

Clay whipped out a newspaper and held it up before the bars. The effect was electrical. Goodloe clutched at his hair and almost reeled backward. Jones uttered an inarticulate, high-pitched growl of horror. For in huge letters, extending across the page was the headline:

BEACH GIRL ESCAPES THE NET

And, underneath:

'The daughter of Cyrus K. Embrich's former partner, and ward of the murdered man, who is now wanted by the police, evades the dragnet and is supposed to be in hiding somewhere within the city.'

Clay quietly handed the paper through the bars. 'Take your time, Mr. Goodloe,' he said suavely. 'Ya see, it really might be best to tell me just what happened, and later, if necessary, we'll get a stenographer from the office to put it into your words over your signature.'

Goodloe, who had been devouring the headlines, flung the paper down with a sudden, nerveless gesture. 'Yes, I'll tell you, Mr. Clay,' he said. 'As you know, Mr. Embrich and I had a quarrel on the afternoon of the day he was murdered. I'd gone down to his office to talk to him, and he was more violent than I have ever known him to be before. I sat at his desk for perhaps twenty minutes, and all the time it was a long tirade against me, partly because Miss Beach had left him, and partly on account of my supposed bad habits of life.

'We'd had quarrels before because the business had failed that he'd started me in. However, this time it seemed a showdown. My uncle was nearly off his head with rage, and he talked unintelligibly about Miss Beach and me having both behaved badly, and that he'd made arrangements to leave his money elsewhere. It meant little to me at the time, but in the light of his secret marriage, of course, it all became plain.

'He didn't give me the chance to say a word, and I knew it would be no use until he'd got over his fit. But I was a good deal worried — not about the money, you understand, but because I felt that matters had come to a crisis. I couldn't continue to live with him, and I wanted us to talk it over calmly and find out where we stood.

'When Peck told me that he was working late at the office I decided to go down and see him that night, and have a definite arrangement before I left. I went down about half past ten —— '

'And you found the door open?' interrupted Clay.

'Wide open. There was nobody about. I went up the back stairs and along the passage to Miss Martin's room. I knew both doors of my uncle's office would be locked, but he'd be in a much better mood if I went in through Miss Martin's office. That was one of his little peculiarities.'

'I know,' said Clay. 'Go on.'

'I knocked two or three times. There was no answer. I tried the handle, and, to my surprise, I saw Miss Beach looking back at me in terror. She screamed, and tried to shut me out. Then over her shoulder I saw my uncle sitting stone dead in his chair, with the blood dripping from his shoulder.' He paused and passed his hand over his damp forehead. 'You understand, I didn't *see* her kill him, and I'm sure she didn't,' he continued. 'I'd swear to it.'

'Just why?' asked Clay softly.

'She — she told me so. I mean, she's not that sort of girl. She — '

'Just a moment,' Clay interrupted. 'Suppose you finish your story, and we'll take up the inferences afterward. What was said then?'

'I can't remember. I was too horrified and overcome. But she told me she'd come to see Mr. Embrich, after telephoning the house and learning that he was going to be at the office late. She'd only been there a minute when I came. She — she was as horrified as me.'

'Quite naturally,' said Clay.

'We saw that nothing could be done, and we agreed that it would be best for us each to go home and say nothing about the murder at all, because our presence there was bound to be connected with it. It seemed to us that no wrong would be done to anyone in that way.'

'And you went out together?'

'I think — no! I went out first and hurried home as fast as I could. You'll realize how shaken I was by the affair. And if it hadn't been for those finger-prints of mine I'd never have been brought into this thing at all.'

'I dunno,' said Clay. 'The girl would've told sooner or later.'

'But I want you to understand,' persisted Goodloe, 'that Miss Beach had no more to do with it than I had. It was just an unlucky accident that brought us both there together.'

'Maybe so. That's out of my province just at present. Anyway, you've made that statement before Mr. Jones and me, and I take it you'll be prepared to put your signature to it this afternoon?'

'I will. I must read it over, of course. How soon will I be allowed to go?'

'Well, we'll do our best for you, Mr. Goodloe,' answered Clay jocosely. 'I guess what you concealed was out of a sense of chivalry to Miss Beach, and that'd weigh with everyone.'

Jones, who had listened with alternat-ing impulses, followed Clay out of the jail in mingled horror and rage. His mind reconstructed the scene; he saw Rosanna discovering the body of the murdered man and marveled at the fortitude and heroism which had sustained her during the awful days that followed when, animated by the sole desire to avenge her guardian's death, she had stuck to her post in full consciousness of her own situation. Never had he felt more convinced of Rosanna's innocence than when he entered the inner sanctum of the homicide bureau with the inspector.

Clay, seating himself, motioned Jones to a chair. Jones, however, remained standing. 'There's no doubt,' mused Clay, 'that young Phil Goodloe's the strongest specimen of a skunk that's crossed my path since they shunted me in here. '*Went first*,' did he? Well, all I can say to that is, either he's lyin', or he's about the lowest specimen of his tribe to leave the girl in that place, murderess or no murderess. What do you think, Mr. Jones?'

'What I think,' said Jones, 'is that you've been playing a damned crooked game.' Honest, tenacious, not to be turned aside, Jones bearded Clay at his desk, expressing the first thought of his fervent soul.

Clay, having lit a cigar, puffed at it leisurely, and then raised his eyes to Jones. 'Ya do, eh?' he asked. 'Well, I'm not altogether surprised at your takin' it that way, human nature bein' what it is. But I did think at first that Vintner had a share in this business, too, and when I learned last night that he'd been in the Night Court at the time the murder was done, it startled me considerably. However, you're in on this case by the express wishes of the late Mr. Embrich. I told you I'd keep you posted on developments. I'll just sum up what evidence there is apart from Goodloe's statement, and ask you what any jury's goin' to make out of it.

'First thing, there was that hand-kerchief. Now, you can see for yourself, Mr. Jones, that's mighty conclusive. Why, I was dead sure it was Jenny's, until Miss Beach asked me that question in the office. As for that subconscious theory of yours, well, I can only take the common sense point of view, and we ain't got to the point yet where the subconscious gets a respectful hearin' in the courts. Is there a single lawyer in the land who'd dare to hang his case upon that subconscious stuff?

'No, sir. Miss Beach was scared out of her wits after she'd stuffed that handkerchief in the pipe in sheer, blind panic, for fear it'd be found. And that touches a curious point in the psychology of murderers. Ya see, Mr. Jones, when they're layin' their lines, it looks convincin'. They fool themselves into thinkin' they've got everybody else fooled. When she bought that handkerchief, she thought it'd be proof positive against Jenny.

'But after she'd rammed it down the waste-pipe she wasn't so sure. She cast about, lookin' for the flaw in the evidence she'd built up. And she got scared. So she put that question to me. She gave herself away cold, and if you didn't suspect her, then all I can say is, give me common sense instead of diagrams.

'Now — second. That hair on Mr. Embrich's shoulder; hers. It's not Jenny's. Maybe Jenny's crop has one or two hairs as yellow as that, but most of it's carroty — and that's a pretty strong presumption, if it ain't proof.

'Third, there's the man Peck. He recognized her voice the minute she spoke to him at Mr. Embrich's house, as havin' been the same that spoke to him over the telephone the night before. And that's goin' some, too.

'Fourth, there's the rubbers. We know the woman who came in by the Fothergill Street store was wearin' rubbers with that pattern. But we find 'em tucked away behind the books on your shelves, which looked as if they hadn't been taken down and dusted since they were put up there.

'Fifth, there's Miss Beach's own actions. Why did she beat it when she saw the game was up? Blind panic.

'Lemme see; that's five points I've given you. I'll give you one more. I don't know whether you observed — most likely you didn't — that when Miss Beach was in Mr. Embrich's office on Wednesday mornin', she leaned back and put her hands against the safe. I saw that, and — well, I've got her fingerprints as clear as any record in the department. And — there was another set of fingerprints on the safe, just about the same place, which wasn't made by Miss Beach that mornin' — because I watched every move she made, and she only put her fingers there once. We've got that second impression, too, and it's the same. It was made not long before — a day, maybe, not more. And how long was it since she'd been into her uncle's office? Weeks, Mr. Jones, weeks!

'When we take that evidence before the jury, together with Phil Goodloe's confession, there won't be the least chance in the world for either. I tell you, Mr. Jones, Rosanna Beach and Phil Goodloe are as guilty as hell. This is the clearest case I've ever handled. It's plain, and the motive's plain, too. The pair of 'em got wise to Mr. Embrich's infatuation for that Adelaide woman. They knew he was proposin' to make her his wife, and — they wanted to keep the property for themselves. Am I right in arrestin' her?'

He slammed his heavy fist down on the desk and glowered at Jones, who, sick with horror, answered, 'From your point of view, yes. But it's not true she murdered him!'

Clay's lips parted in a sneering grin. 'Oh, come, Mr. Jones, that ain't bein' fair to our profession!' he said. 'Ya can't catch murderers with silk gloves, not murderesses either. But I'll take that from just one man, and that's you, knowin' you're *sweet* on her.'

★ ★ ★

Three days had passed since Jones's last interview with Clay. They had been days of anguish during which he had devoured every edition of the newspapers, dreading to read news of Rosanna's arrest.

Vintner, charged with a minor offense, had unexpectedly obtained his release on bail through the intervention of some unknown person. Jenny had been set free. Goodloe's reputed 'confession' was known, and public opinion howled for the capture of the girl who, in its belief, had conspired with her lover to murder their common guardian for a sordid end.

And Jones came in for a good deal of unwelcome attention. He was depicted as a cunning criminal or an ingenuous ass. His system was made the subject of caricatures. He was spied on by the press and shadowed by detectives.

Jones cared very little for all this. Remaining at home by day, he made his way down to his office nightly, and there sat wrestling with his variables till dawn. He had explored them all with his dogged pertinacity, and he had gone as far as pure mathematics could lead him. A woman *had* murdered Embrich. A man *had* been associated with her in some inexplicable way, and yet had had *no hand* in the slaying. And the motive was neither robbery nor revenge.

He had gone nightly to Madison Square to receive Bobby's report, but he had never seen Bobby, and he had abandoned all hope of it. He had not a doubt that the boy had quickly tired of playing detective and had gone back to his old stand near headquarters, where Jones was no longer welcome.

The decision which Jones had now

reached was a momentous one for him. It was nothing less than to abandon further mathematical investigations and to adopt the practical role, despite his lack of all the qualities of the detective. He resolved to follow up the Timson clue. Also he decided, as a preliminary, to see Miss Martin.

Accordingly, he proceeded to the small hotel at which she lived and, sending up his card, was presently admitted to her two rooms on the seventh floor.

Miss Martin's appearance shocked Jones. She was in a negligee, her hair hastily wound up in a ball at the back of her head, and she looked generally disheveled and unkempt. The suave, comely secretary, the embodiment of almost masculine neatness formerly, was now hardly recognizable in this gaunt, haggard woman with the blue half-circles beneath her eyes, hollow cheeks and sagging skin that was covered with a network of tiny wrinkles.

Only her self-possessed manner remained. 'Come in, Mr. Jones,' she said quietly, ushering him. She sat down with a sudden, weak collapse of muscular power,

211

and motioned him to take a chair. 'I've hardly slept since this terrible development,' she added in a harsh, unsteady voice. 'And I'm nearly mad with anxiety. They won't let me see Philip. It's a *fake*!' she went on hysterically. 'That supposed confession. He never confessed. And why should they keep me from him?'

'I was present with Clay when he made his statement,' said Jones. 'It was no confession, but he admitted having been down to the office, and having seen Mr. Embrich's body in the chair, and Miss Beach standing beside it.'

Miss Martin looked almost demented. 'Then he — he was *there*?' she gasped.

'He had gone to speak to his uncle. He denied all knowledge of the murderer.'

'Then who *was* it?' Miss Martin cried. 'Who but Vintner? And they've let *him* out on bail.' She burst into loud, mocking laughter.

'Miss Martin, have you suspicions of anyone other than Vintner who might have been interested in Mr. Embrich's death?' asked Jones.

The abrupt cessation of the laughter

was more startling than its beginning. The secretary was as still as an image. Only her eyes turned on Jones and transfixed him. 'Oh, it *was* Vintner!' she cried. 'How many times must I attempt to make you men see the obvious? Nobody else bore Mr. Embrich anything but love.'

'The evidence against Vintner — ' began Jones.

'Is absolute,' she interrupted. 'He alone had the motive. He had threatened Mr. Embrich. And I saw him skulking in the yard that day with my own eyes. Then there's that Friend woman, his sweetheart and accomplice. Her handkerchief, with blood on it! In heaven's name, how could they let *her* go?' She went on with a passionate gesture, 'Do you wonder to see me looking like *this?* And I know — a woman does know by instinct, Mr. Jones, and doesn't need to weigh each scrap of evidence; though, goodness knows, that's overwhelming!'

'But, still, Miss Martin, the evidence that Vintner was under arrest in the Night Court at the time the autopsy shows the murder to have been committed seems almost unassailable. It is testified to, remember, by the patrolman who arrested him. Now, under those circumstances, what could Clay do but — '

Miss Martin leaped to her feet. 'Oh, I tell you Vintner *killed* Mr. Embrich!' she cried, in almost uncontrollable excitement. 'Mr. Embrich retained your services before his death, as if he foresaw what was going to happen. What do you believe? Do you think in your heart that Philip Goodloe is innocent?'

'I am absolutely convinced,' said Jones emphatically, 'that Philip Goodloe no more struck the blow which killed Mr. Embrich than Miss Beach did.'

'You — you are sure that Miss Beach mightn't have — have done it in uncontrollable anger?' asked the secretary, looking at Jones in a curious manner.

Jones realized what an astounding change of front this was. At the moment a gust of furious anger overcame him at the idea that Miss Martin was trying to sacrifice Rosanna to save her favorite.

'So far as I can see,' said Jones, 'except for Mr. Goodloe's statement that he was in the office, there is no evidence against him beyond his fingerprints upon the envelope-opener. Their presence he has explained. But that counts heavily with a jury. As for Miss Beach, I know that she is innocent.'

Miss Martin was staring at Jones with a rapt look. Her eyes were preternaturally bright and, as if evoked by his mental cry for enlightenment, some speech that would solve his perplexities appeared to tremble on her tongue.

'Miss Martin, if you know anything bearing on all this, anything that would throw a new light on it, won't you tell me — in confidence, if necessary — to clear Philip Goodloe and Miss Beach?' asked Jones.

Miss Martin took an impulsive step toward him. 'Oh, if you knew — ' she began, and then there came a ring at the doorbell. Uttering a suppressed exclamation, Miss Martin held up her hand, either for silence or to detain him there, and went into the tiny hall. Jones heard the door open, Miss Martin's sharp exclamation, and then a man's voice.

The back of the secretary was partly visible through the half-closed door, and a moment later Jones saw a man push Miss Martin coolly aside, stride to the door, and stand looking at him.

It was the butler, Peck — smooth, furtive, silent, sneering, and looking defiantly at Jones through his half-closed eyelids. Without a word, the man swung about and pulled the door shut with a movement that conveyed an impression of indescribable insolence.

The colloquy went on interminably, the butler's droning voice and Miss Martin's occasional high-toned protests. 'Tomorrow night!' Jones heard her repeat sharply. Minutes passed before Jones heard Peck walk away along the passage.

Miss Martin came back into the room. Her face was deadly white, her voice hard and full of resolution. 'I must ask you to go immediately, Mr. Jones,' she said. 'You have brought me no information, and I cannot see you further.'

'I wanted — ' Jones began, but she turned upon him with a fierce gesture.

'Will you *go?*' she demanded. 'I'm too

216

ill to be persecuted in this way. Isn't the police department more than any woman can stand, without you amateurs poking your noses in here? Go at once, and don't come bothering me again!'

Jones went out, and Miss Martin, hardly waiting till he was in the corridor, closed her door with a vicious slam.

Peck was waiting at the elevator, which was coming up the shaft. As Jones approached him he gave him his quick, furtive look, but said nothing at the moment. They went down together, and at the entrance to the hotel Peck turned his head sidewise.

'You keep out of this, or it will be worse for you!' he mumbled through half-closed lips.

12

Jones paid no attention to the fellow, but proceeded slowly uptown, trying to puzzle out the meaning of the morning's interview. It was plain to him that Miss Martin might have told him something which would have had a vital bearing upon the mystery. It was also plain that Peck's advent had turned her from her purpose.

The man's presence and power in the Embrich house was itself a mystery, and it was likely that in some way Peck had acquired an influence over Miss Martin. Yet, on the other hand, this might simply be due to his knowledge of family affairs; or he might be in possession of some secret not necessarily relative to the murder.

His mind whirling, Jones turned his thoughts to Timson. The assistant manager and Embrich had been secret partners in a manner of life that one usually pursues alone; a bitter animosity had existed on Timson's part against his employer, while Embrich had clearly condoned Timson's alias as Sanford Rogers.

Jones decided to call on Timson. The store being still closed, it would be necessary to go to his apartment. He stepped into a drugstore and looked up Timson in the telephone book. He found that the address was not in the Bronx, but in Harlem, and took an uptown subway train, getting off some twenty minutes later at One Hundred and Twenty-Fifth Street.

As was likely enough in the case of a man who spent his money as Timson did, the address proved to be an unpretentious apartment in a house without an elevator. Repeated ringing failed to elicit the familiar *click-click* of the door latch.

At last Jones rang the janitor's bell, and presently a pleasant, matronly woman opened the door. 'The Timsons? Why, they ain't here no more!' exclaimed the woman after Jones had stated the purpose of his visit. 'Left nearly a week ago, the wife and kids did. The apartment's been rented from next Monday.'

'Where?' asked Jones.

The woman shrugged her shoulders expressively. 'Where should she go with five children and a husband like that?' she asked. 'She ain't gone with *him*, I'll bet that! A bad lot, that's what I call that man. Kept 'em short of pretty nearly everything, and quarrels — ' She threw up her hands. 'More'n once I seen her with a black eye,' she said. 'I've seen her crying, too, when Mr. Timson hadn't been home all night. I guess she'd have left him long ago if it wasn't for the children. Pretty little thing she were, but worn-looking. No, I've no idea where she's gone, but I wish I'd had the manhandling of him!'

Jones withdrew with the feeling that the whole quest was hopeless. He took a train downtown but, as it neared Forty-Second Street, it occurred to him as a possibility that Adelaide Embrich might have some further news of Sanford Rogers. Accordingly, changing into a local, he got out at Twenty-Third Street and proceeded to her apartment.

Since he had seen her, Jones had come

to regard her as being entirely identified with himself and Rosanna, so far as the investigation was concerned. He was disconcerted, therefore, by the coolness of his reception.

'*Really*, this is *quite* unexpected, Mr. Jones!' the girl began. 'I think you might at *least* have telephoned me. As it happens, I am extremely busy this morning. What is it I can do for you?'

'I'm sorry to have intruded,' said Jones. 'I merely wished to ask if you have heard anything more about Sanford Rogers.'

'I have not!'

'I understood that you were going to — '

'Quite so! But that was before this new turn of affairs.'

'Surely, Mrs. Embrich, you don't mean to insinuate that Miss Beach is — is *guilty*?' Jones demanded in amazement.

'My dear man, it is not my business to insinuate anything,' she returned with asperity. 'I have troubles enough of my own, without taking other people's burdens on my shoulders.' Then, softening a little, she added, 'Of course, it must be something of a shock to you to find Miss Beach involved so gravely in this horrible affair,' she said.

'*Mrs.* *Embrich*,' Jones protested hotly, 'if you have got it into your head that Ros — that Miss Beach can possibly be guilty, please drive it out again. I *know* that girl. She's pure gold, and absolutely incapable of such a dastardly crime.'

'Indeed?' asked Adelaide Embrich, looking at him with a curious smile. 'The case against her seems a bit strong, if the newspapers are at all correct.'

'I tell you that she is *incapable* of such a crime,' cried Jones, beginning to lose his temper.

'Pretty strong talk,' commented Adelaide. 'I should say that you were in love with her, Mr. Jones.'

'In so far as I'm fit to breathe the same air she breathes, I certainly *am*,' said Jones. 'And that's why I'm going to free her and Philip Goodloe.'

'Oh! Why Phil Goodloe, pray?'

'Because they love each other and want to get married.'

Adelaide laughed merrily. 'Really, you

are very naïve, Mr. Jones!' she said. 'It's quite refreshing to meet such disinterested love nowadays.'

Jones turned toward the door, turned back, and shook his huge fist in the amazed girl's face.

'I wonder how you'll feel when Miss Beach returns — a *free* woman!' he shouted. 'I pity you when you meet!'

Adelaide, not in the least dismayed, caught him by the shoulders and attempted valiantly to push him toward the door. 'Oh, you quixotic, foolish man! Go away, now!' she said.

Shrugging his shoulders, Jones went, and reached his office a quarter of an hour later the slouching embodiment of defeat.

He was not cut out to be a detective. Before Rosanna came he had always cooperated with some detective agency which had handled the practical side, or had had as an employer someone capable himself of putting his theoretical deductions to practical advantage.

In deep despondency he sat down and began a new super-series of noughts and crosses. He had played half a game when he heard a girl's steps on the stairs. She was coming toward his office. His heart began to hammer. He had a wild hope it was Rosanna.

But it was not Rosanna's footsteps, neither was that her tap. He straightened himself. 'Come in!' he called.

Jenny Friend entered. The girl came up to Jones without a word, drew out a chair, and sat down. Her face was thickly powdered, there was a touch of carmine on her lips, and she gave the appearance of having been celebrating her release from jail by a general relaxation of her former decorum in dress.

When she began to speak Jones perceived that she was trying to smother her extreme agitation. 'Yer workin' on this case, aren't ya?' she asked.

Jones nodded a thin-lipped affirmation.

'Nor ya don't love Clay more than ya have to, I guess,' Jenny continued. 'I could see that, the way ya looked at him. And I doped it out ya wouldn't mind getting Miss Beach out of Clay's clutches. Well, I got nothin' against her, and Mr. Embrich was mighty good to me and mother.'

'What do you know?' Jones almost shouted in his elation.

But her next words dashed his hopes. 'Nothin' about who croaked him — nothin' for sure. Exceptin' that it wasn't her, nor Phil Goodloe, either. Phil hasn't the heart of a rat. Lord, to think of him croakin' anybody!' She put her elbows on the table and leaned forward, and her face quivered with passion. 'No, I don't know who killed Mr. Embrich, and that's straight goods. But I'll tell you the name of the blackest cur I know. It's Timson! I haven't been in the office long, but I kept my eyes open, and I got wise to a thing or two. Remember that case Vintner was in, when they sent him up the river?'

Jones nodded.

'Well, there was more than Vintner to that. And that more's also called Timson. I got wise to the fact that somebody was in with Vintner in them thefts of his. Name: Timson! Don't forget it!' cried Jenny. 'I got no evidence to give. I'm simply putting ya wise to what was going on. Listen, Mr. Jones, and I'll tell ya some more!

'Timson took me out to supper. Oh, yes, I'd been going with him a lot, but he'd begun to find I wasn't the kind he thought I was, and he said, pretendin' to joke — but I knew he meant it — he said I could get ten thousand bucks out of the old man if I'd say so-and-so — ya *know* what I mean — and that, because of the reputation he had, the old man would pay up rather than fight it.

'Course I turned him down cold on that prop. Then Vintner come out of the pen, mad, because he'd been made the goat over that stealing. And he got wise to me going out with Timson, and he didn't like that one bit, either. And what do ya suppose? Timson fixed up a deal with him, payin' him something, and turnin' me over to him as part and parcel of it. What do ya think of *that* — a man what'd promised to *marry* me!

'Yes, Timson'd promised to marry me, and on the strength of that I didn't let out one bleat when Clay hooked me, not even when they flashed that phony handkerchief on me. And I found that he's a married man with five kids!

'Well, I'm nobody's goat, and, if ya want to follow up what I've been tellin' ya, I'm going to put ya wise. They's a place down near Eleventh Avenue where Vintner hangs out. I guess it's one of these dens of iniquity the papers tell about now and then.'

'Where is it? Can you show me?' Jones asked eagerly.

'Say,' began the girl, shuddering. 'I was there once long ago, before Vintner was sent up. I guess he'd put some dope in the wine he gave me, or somethin' — anyway, he wanted me to go in and see his mother, and I took one glint and beat it. You don't catch *me* goin' there again. But I'll tell *you* how to get there!'

★ ★ ★

It was undeniably absurd for Jones to have disguised himself with a false mustache of ebony hue and a black wig. In his defense, he was under the illusion that such accessories were a necessary part of the detective's stock in trade.

Analyzing Jenny's story, he believed the

men who had been plundering the store were the authors of Embrich's murder. He had thrown mathematics to the wind and had forgotten all about the curve of obscure causes. Also, with an intuition remarkable in him, he had connected Peck's words 'tomorrow night' to Miss Martin with this haunt of the gang, and had jumped to the conclusion that there would be something doing that evening at the place on Eleventh Avenue.

He reconnoitered the place that afternoon, and was astonished at its appearance. It was an old building, condemned as unsafe and marked for demolition. The whole block was to be torn down, for workmen had been demolishing nearby, and the entire weed-grown terrain was strewn with beams, joists, debris of bricks and a miscellany of rubbish. The building was enclosed in a dilapidated wooden fence, the farther side of which abutted on the railroad tracks, and the aspect of the whole was the dreariest imaginable.

More foolish than the disguise was Jones' recklessness in going alone. Despite the automatic in his pocket, Jones was altogether devoid of fear. His precise mind never painted pictures of possibilities. If he could have visualized himself lying dead, face upward to the rainy skies in that rubbish yard where a body might lie for days before discovery, Jones would have laughed and gone on his way.

How he was going to proceed, Jones had not the least idea. Bull-headed, lion-hearted, and ugly as sin in his black wig and ebony mustache, Jones made his lonely way toward Vintner's scatter.

By night the place was even more depressing and squalid. Skulkers loitered at dismal corners, bound on some errand of darkness; but once he had scrambled through a gap in the fence, Jones found himself utterly alone. The dank smell of decaying vegetation and rotting refuse came thickly to his nostrils.

There was a rumble and a stream of shifting light as a train made its way along the tracks beyond the building.

Jones, having reached the place, stood looking at it. He began to doubt whether Peck's words to Miss Martin had been interpreted by him correctly. There was no light, no sign of life about the gloomy place.

The entrance was by a flight of dilapidated wooden steps that led up to a creaking door. Jones ascended and pushed it back, to the accompaniment of a volley of groaning protests. Within the cavernous blackness he descried a flight of wooden stairs. He began to make his way up a flight; every step creaked noisily beneath his feet. The whole building seemed to quiver and shake at the least footfall. Once, when another train rumbled past, it seemed to shake to its foundation, and fragments of moldy plaster fell in a hail.

Reaching the second landing, Jones stopped and looked about him. There were three doors on this floor, just discernible by the light that came through the hall window, but only darkness was visible through the wide chinks left by the sagging panels. Looking upward, however, Jones saw a very slight and diffused radiance at a flight above him, such as might come from a light streaming under a door.

On tiptoe he began the negotiation of the next flight. The walls were mottled with fungoid growths. Once, when a board gave beneath his feet with a crash which echoed through the house, Jones stopped; he listened nearly a minute before continuing his journey.

Arrived at the top of this flight, he discovered the source of the illumination. As he had surmised, it came from beneath a door facing him at the end of a short corridor. As he stopped, he fancied that he heard the stairs creak beneath him.

Even Jones's nerves began to give at his surroundings and, placing his hand upon the automatic in his pocket, he drew back against the wall, trying to peer down through the gaps in the rotting balusters. Once more he fancied he heard the creak, but it was not repeated.

At length, reassured, he turned toward the room with the light, from which came the faint hum of voices. In this passage the boards were firmer, and gave out no sound under his feet. Very softly Jones advanced, until he was within a few paces of the door, where was the embrasure of a window, the lower part shuttered, the upper broken glass through which could be seen the city lights.

The door was the least bit ajar, and the room appeared to be lit, but only a small strip of the wall was visible. Then a shadow began to move upon it. There was a hum of inaudible voices. The shadow was talking, too; the mouth opened and closed.

It was the butler, Peck, in silhouette.

As Jones stood back against the embrasure his heel scraped noisily against a protruding nail. Instantly the shadow turned.

'What's *that*?' demanded a shrill, startled voice, which Jones recognized as Timson's.

'*Rats!* Cut it out!' came Peck's voice contemptuously. 'Say, you give me the willies, the way you jump!'

There was nothing of the smooth butler about Peck now. His voice was the hardest and ugliest that Jones had ever heard. The shadow loomed gigantic on the wall, faded, and Peck's face appeared at the door. The butler, looking out, was within a fist's strike of Jones; but hidden in the darkness of the recess, crouching with his head beneath the half-drawn lower shutter of the window, he was completely invisible.

Peck went back. 'Nothing doing!' he said.

'See here,' said Timson. 'You know we're in a devil of a hole, Peck? The auditors may issue their report any time now, and they're keeping so infernally quiet I guess they're hard at work tracing the responsibility for the defalcations.' He laughed. 'Sixty thousand makes quite a hole in the Embrich stock-in-trade,' he said. 'If it wasn't that the murder has eclipsed the matter of the auditing, we might as well have cut and run for it as soon as Vintner killed the old man.'

Jones started. He could hardly believe his ears. But Timson's voice went calmly on: 'Thank God we got the last of the stuff out of the warehouse yesterday. That was smart work of yours, I must say. It's ruinous, the price we had to sell for. It's all right for you, Peck, as a sort of

233

sleeping partner; but it's been hell for me, having to show myself every day to let them think, in case they do suspect me.'

'I dunno,' growled Peck. 'I thought at one time that Jones guy had a sort of suspicion, the way he looked at me. But I guess the girl's flight busted that partnership, so far as Clay's concerned, anyway. Where in hell's Vintner? Say, if he tries to pull anything about them securities he'll never leave this joint alive — say! What was that?'

This time there was no mistaking the alarm on Timson's face, nor that reflected on the butler's. Peck leaped softly to his feet and flung the door wide open.

The opened door, which concealed Jones completely, had all but struck him in the face. He drew his automatic very softly from his pocket, holding his breath for fear of betraying his presence. Only a half-inch of paneling separated him from Peck and Timson.

He could see nothing at all in the passage, but through the widened crack of the door Jones could see the whole squalid interior of the room — the bed, the table with three chairs, the cheap lamp, the strip of oilcloth, and a bulging bag flung down upon the floor.

Then he heard a sigh of relief from the two men, and for an instant at the edge of the door, he saw a face, ghastly pale, and eyes brilliant in its whiteness.

'You gave us a bit of a scare, Miss Martin!' Timson grumbled. 'Say, you're mighty late; I was thinking maybe you'd changed your mind about coming.'

He shot a keen look at her, but Miss Martin did not answer him, and Timson turned back into the room.

'Sit down, Miss Martin,' said Timson ungraciously, handing her a chair. 'Vintner'll be along presently.'

Miss Martin remained silent. Jones had not heard her sit down. She or somebody in the room was breathing in great, hoarse gasps that vibrated like the scission of a saw.

The flood of light from the open door had dulled the sensibility of Jones's retinas, so that the faint illumination diffused from the window and around the door had given place to complete darkness. Jones, staring out into it, could see nothing, and even the strip of wall with Peck's shadow upon it had become indistinct and wavering before his eyes.

And as he turned his ears toward the drama in the room, he heard further creaking down below.

13

Vintner came quickly along the passage. When he entered the room and saw the three waiting for him, a rumble like a wild beast's growl came from his throat. He stood in the doorway, surveying them. 'Well, you damn double-crossers!' he snarled. 'You're going to come across clean before I've done with you! I've got the dope on you, Timson. You'll pay for making me the goat, by God!'

Timson attempted to take him by the arm, but Vintner wrenched himself free. 'For heaven's sake, don't shout like that!' pleaded the manager. 'This is our last meeting. Everything's fixed, and I've got the money here. Let's divvy it up and beat it!'

'You betcha!' snorted Vintner. 'And I'm in the place where I can watch it being done. I seen that fence, Baravitch, and I guess he's let out pretty well what he's paid for them stolen goods from first to last. I ain't no fool, Timson!'

He growled in his throat. '*Say!* What've I got out of this deal since the beginning?' he snarled. 'You're a bright lot if you think you're going to four-flush me!'

His voice broke off in rattles. Vintner was drunk, fighting drunk. The manager intervened once more: 'Let's get to business instead of raising Cain. We've met to divvy up equally. Put down the securities and whatever else you got from Embrich's safe, and we'll empty the bag. I've got the cash here.'

Across the shadow of Peck's face on the wall swept the orbit of Vintner's head, obliterating it.

'Whatjermean, 'put down them securities'?' cried Vintner furiously. 'Who's got 'em?'

'Who's got them? Who'd have them but *you*?' cried Peck. 'You got them and planted them somewhere, didn't you? Who else'd have 'em? Wasn't they left in the safe in Embrich's office, as arranged for?'

'How'd I know?' inquired Vintner ferociously.

'Well,' sneered Peck, 'seeing that you croaked the old man, I naturally supposed you hadn't been too absent-minded to stop to pick up the fruit.'

'Me croaked him?' Vintner fairly yelled. 'Why, I wasn't never in Embrich's office in my life!' And he raged, spitting out blasphemies. 'What sort of game are you trying to put on me now?' he shouted. 'Say, don't you guys read the papers? Didn't you read I was in the Night Court when Embrich croaked? How'd it be me? How'd I know about the damn securities? Whoever killed him's got 'em. I guessed it was *you*, Peck!'

He laughed viciously. 'Say, that game won't work!' he jeered. 'I guess you know where them securities are!'

Peck started toward him, but Miss Martin leaped at Vintner as if she would tear him. 'You're *lying*!' she shrilled. 'You killed Mr. Embrich! You thought I'd get those securities from the bank and stuff the safe with them, and bills, too, to fill your pockets, you blackmailers, didn't you? Well, that's where you fooled yourselves! That safe was empty all the time!' She turned upon Vintner. 'You *fool*,' she screamed, 'you murdered Mr. Embrich for nothing at all, and you'll never put it on Phil Goodloe! You'll go to the chair first, if I have to swear my own life away!'

With an oath Vintner leaped at her and hurled her to the floor. The woman struggled like a maniac, still screaming at the top of her voice. She fought Vintner on her knees, tearing with her nails at his face.

Jones sprang from his hiding place. At the sudden sight of him Vintner momentarily released his hold of the secretary. Miss Martin, springing to her feet, ran screaming from the room. Vintner and Peck flung themselves at Jones, but recoiled at the sight of the automatic in his hand.

'Guess the game's up, friends!' As he spoke, he kept the weapon more or less covering both Peck and Vintner, so as to turn it on either at the instant of attack. Timson, in the background, he considered a coward, and ignored as a possible assailant. In that judgment he erred.

Timson bobbed suddenly. A hidden pistol barked.

Jones's right arm dropped to his side. His automatic thudded upon the floor. Instantly the two ruffians were upon him, pinioning his arms, kicking him, hammering at his head with the butt ends of their weapons. Only his wig and the thin shield of his sound arm protected him.

He fought with his utmost fury. A stunning blow momentarily dazed him. Mechanically he fought off their assault, hearing Timson shouting about Miss Martin. It happened so quickly that he could still hear the secretary's footsteps upon the stairs. Jones was still fighting hard when Timson stole up on him and drove his heel into his chest. Then he collapsed backward.

Another blow from the butt of Vintner's pistol descended, cutting his scalp and deluging him with blood. A black cloud of unconsciousness began to envelop him.

Jones's next sensation was of being carried down the stairs. The cold night air blew on him. He became vaguely aware

241

that he was lying upon the ground. But he was too weak to move. He groaned and sank into semi-consciousness.

The ground vibrated and shook. A rumble filled the air. Out of the yards a fiery monster, gathering speed, came swooping toward him.

Between his flickering eyelids Jones saw Death approaching.

* * *

Voices shouting in his ears roused Jones from his lethargy.

He opened his eyes. The headlights of the engine were almost upon him; the roar seemed to fill the whole universe. The sleepers quivered as if on springs.

Then he was seized by the shoulders and pulled from the metals. He rolled upon the gravel inter-track, while the steel monster ground out its passage over the spot where he had been lying.

He heard a thankful cry, and a woman sobbing. He looked blearily up into the faces of Bobby Mann and — Rosanna!

Rosanna crouched beside him, shaken

and trembling. Her tears fell on his face. Bobby, at the other side of him, was grinning foolishly.

Jones raised himself with an immense effort. He was recovering rapidly, but everything was whirling around him. A fearful, stabbing pain was creeping into his numbed arm, and his head felt as it if were being clamped by huge steel pincers while a huge blacksmith hammered it on his anvil.

Jones stirred feebly, and Rosanna drew his head upon her knee and began wiping away the clotted blood about his eyes. 'It's all right!' she whispered brokenly. 'It's all right! Thank Heaven we were just in time!'

'They — ' gasped Jones, pointing toward the tenement, 'they murdered — '

'The police got them. A woman called the police. They were arrested as they were trying to escape. I saw it. Lie still!'

Her speech was almost as disjointed as Jones's. When she had wiped the blood from his face, Rosanna caught sight of his wounded arm. Uttering a low cry, she began to rip up the sleeve with a pen knife that Bobby passed to her. It had stopped bleeding and, convinced of this, the girl tore off a strip from the hem of her petticoat and bound Jones's arm to his breast. When she had finished she asked anxiously, 'How do you feel? We must get you away. Could you manage to walk a few yards, if Bobby and I support you?'

'I'm — as — fit — as a — lark,' answered Jones, trying hard to grin.

Rosanna looked at him dubiously and shook her head. 'I've got a car down behind the fence,' she said. 'I don't think the police suspect you're here. But they mustn't catch us.'

'Good Lord, no!' muttered Jones. 'You must — get away, Rosanna! I dunno how you — police want you. Must have seen newspapers — '

Rosanna whispered to Bobby, and the two of them, with great difficulty, hoisted Jones upon his feet. He stood reeling under a circling sky. He gripped Rosanna's shoulder hard to save himself from falling. Jones began to stumble a few feet at a time toward the hidden car.

Once he stopped, gripping the fence. 'Where — we going?' he demanded.

'I'm going to take you to Adelaide's apartment,' answered Rosanna. 'Can you walk just a few paces further?' she added to Jones.

'*You* can't,' Jones muttered. 'Not to — *there* — '

'You mean Adelaide?'

'Yes. Can't go there. I'll tell you — when I get stronger. Take you down to the office.'

'Oh, we *must* go there,' pleaded Rosanna, looking in dismay at the stubborn, ghastly face that Jones turned on her.

'You — don't understand, Rosanna. That woman's — ' said Jones with an effort. 'I went to see her. She said you were — murderess. She'll betray you. Don't trust her!'

Rosanna clung to him, sobbing and laughing hysterically. 'Oh, it's all right, I promise. You don't understand. I'll explain to you. Just come! Won't you come, for my sake? See, there's the car!'

Clinging to him, coaxing, urging, with Bobby propping him up manfully on the other side, Rosanna got Jones to where the car began to be discernible at the edge of the road, almost concealed by the sloping ground and overhanging fence. She got in, after helping Jones to a seat. Bobby followed, and the car began to glide softly past the gloomy pile toward the avenue.

As they rounded the corner a figure leaped forward and shouted, hand uplifted. The man's shouts died away upon the wind. A crack of his pistol was followed by the splintering of glass and the seat between Rosanna and Jones. But in the dark it was impossible for the patrolman to have read the plate number.

In a few minutes they were gliding easily along Broadway. They made the run to the apartment. Leaving Bobby to run the car round to the garage, Rosanna set herself to the task of helping Jones up the many flights of stairs. This task proved less formidable than had been expected. Though his head still ached violently, and his wounded arm throbbed feverishly, Jones was now fairly steady; he made the long climb leaning on the girl's arm, and at last they stopped before Adelaide's apartment.

Rosanna, who had pressed the bell below, now rang again. In a moment Adelaide was at the open door, gazing with startled eyes at Jones.

'We got him just in time,' said Rosanna.

Adelaide suppressed the little cry that rose to her lips and, putting her arm round Jones's waist, helped lead him into her little living room. The two women got him to the lounge.

'Now, Mr. Jones, I'm going to do whatever's necessary,' said Adelaide. 'I served nine months as a Red Cross nurse, so you're safe in my hands.'

And she produced gauze bandages and bound his head; she removed his coat with infinite care, ripped off the sleeve of the shirt, and washed the wound, afterward examining it critically.

'That bullet went clean between your ulna and radius, Mr. Jones, and came out the other side,' she said. 'Nothing's broken, thank goodness. Now I'm going to give you a drink and put you to bed.'

'I *won't* go to bed,' said Jones, like a schoolboy. 'See here, I'm going to talk straight to you. Last time I was here you called Ros — Miss Beach a murderess. At least, you suggested it.' He was surprised to see the two women exchange amused glances.

'Oh, you big, stupid man. I've got no patience with you!' answered Adelaide. 'That was to get rid of you when you came bothering here at inconvenient hours.'

'Yes, but see here,' Jones expostulated, as Adelaide began to mix something from a black bottle, 'there's no time to be wasted. I know you've given up your job, Miss Beach, but — I tell you I know the murderers. Are you sure the police took them away?'

'Dead sure,' said Rosanna. 'Anyway — is he fit to hear, Adelaide?'

'If he drinks this all down and lies very still, maybe,' said Adelaide, putting the tumbler to Jones's lips. Jones obeyed her. He made a wry face, for he was of strictly teetotal habits.

'Anyway, I was saying that I saw Peck and Timson,' Rosanna continued. 'And there was someone else — I couldn't distinguish him in the dark.'

'Vintner,' said Jones. 'If they've got all three, our chase has come to an end. Vintner killed Mr. Embrich, but it was more or less arranged among the gang, I guess. I'm sorry it was so, because it means the final end of my mathematical system. However, farming's the ideal life, and — '

'Oh, Mr. Jones, if you'd only hold your horses!' Rosanna interrupted. 'Don't forget what happened when you got after Vintner before! Now, do let me go on. I'd just got the car cached under that fence when the patrolmen got them. Pretty smart work! They were coming out one by one, and it was one — two — three — Heavens, the way those handcuffs sounded! They got a woman, too. She was in hysterics. I wasn't near enough to get it all, but I'm positive I recognized Peck and Timson.'

'What were you there for?' Jones inquired.

'Oh, I just happened to be taking a ride, and my subconscious intuition, as you call it, warned me — ' She broke off in convulsive laughter, which was rather the reaction from the experiences of the evening than inspired by mirth.

'Mr. Jones,' she said, 'I do believe that, off paper, you are the worst detective in the world. Look at him, Adelaide!'

Adelaide stepped back and, looking Jones in the face, burst into helpless laughter. She sobbed, rocking herself to and fro. 'It only struck me as queer this minute.'

She held a mirror before Jones's face with shaking fingers. Upon his upper lip Jones saw the bristling, furious mustache of a Sicilian brigand. He tore off his disguise and flung it across the room, wondering what spirit of deviltry had taken hold of the girls.

'I'm going on. Can he hear more?'

'If he — yes, if you don't excite him too much,' said Adelaide, surveying the patient.

'Well, Mr. Jones, I really think you've got all the detective masters of fiction beat to a frazzle,' Rosanna went on. 'Do you know you've been shadowed every minute for three days past?'

'I suppose so. Those newspapers — '

'It wasn't the newspapers — at least, it was somebody else, too.'

'You, Ro — Miss Beach?'

'No. Bobby Mann.'

'*Bobby Mann?*' cried Jones. 'Why, you told him to shadow Sanford Rogers!'

'I know, but we didn't need to after we found out who Sanford Rogers is, did we?'

'Why did you set him on me?'

'Because I knew — I just knew, Mr. Jones, that you'd do something rash! Bobby saw you go into that tenement. He saw a lady enter. Then he telephoned me at once — I had a car on order at the garage the moment I might need it. He knew something was wrong. He thought — you must forgive him, because he's had a different sort of experience of life — he thought the lady had lured you there to rob you.

'When Bobby met me at the corner, he said he thought he'd seen two men carrying a bundle toward the railway tracks. He couldn't keep watch very well from across the street. But I took the chance, and — well, I found you!'

'You've saved my life, Miss Beach,' said Jones. 'But wasn't it risky of you to go about New York with half the town looking for you?'

'No,' answered Rosanna coolly. 'I'm going down to headquarters in the morning to surrender.'

'But, Ros — Miss Beach, do you realize how strong the case against you seems to be?' asked Jones. 'We must first make sure we can convict the murderer. We must know who it is.'

'Adelaide,' said Rosanna, ignoring Jones, 'could your patient possibly come down to headquarters in a cab in the morning?'

'We'll see — if he goes straight to bed,' Adelaide answered.

14

The arrival of the party of three on the following morning created a crescendo of excitement. Rosanna was arrested simultaneously by four policemen. Four captors escorted the party into Clay's sanctuary.

Miss Martin was sitting placidly upon a chair beside his desk. She had become the well-trained secretary once more. Even the entrance of the party failed to stir her to do more than turn her head and glance indifferently at them.

As for Clay, he merely raised his eyebrows and said, with a colossal demonstration of nerve, 'Mornin', Jones! Mornin', Miss Beach! Glad to see you back on the job again. And Mrs. Embrich, I believe. Pleased to have you throw any further light you can upon this subject, I'm sure.'

He nodded dismissal to the attendant policemen, who withdrew in surprise and chagrin, and, rising, placed chairs for all the party, seating them in such a position that the light shone on their faces. Then he turned to Miss Martin. 'Let me see. You'd begun to make a statement to me?' he asked casually.

'I was saying,' answered the secretary in her well-modulated voice, 'that *I* am responsible for the murder of Cyrus Embrich.'

'Yes, I got that,' replied the inspector blandly. 'But I think I was askin' you about these defalcations in the store which the auditors found at the time you told me that. Suppose we keep to the one track first. You and the three persons arrested last night, and the fence — Baravitch — were all mixed up in that game, I believe? Anyone else?'

'Nobody else, to my knowledge,' Miss Martin answered. 'And I wish it clearly understood that I never touched a penny of it.'

'Quite so,' said Clay. 'And how long had this been goin' on?'

'A year at least. Vintner was acting as disposer of the goods. I knew all about the affair at the time of his arrest.'

'You gave evidence in the court to the contrary,' suggested Clay.

'I did,' answered Miss Martin quietly.

'Well, touchin' on the murder, now, I'll be glad to have you amplify that statement you made.'

'You shall have it quite frankly,' Miss Martin answered in her easy way. 'Vintner murdered Mr. Embrich in the course of robbing the safe of a number of securities and large bills which I had left there, instead of depositing them in the bank. I understand that a death occurring through the committing of a felony is equivalent to murder, according to the laws of the State of New York, not merely on the part of the actual murderer, but also on the part of all who are engaged in the conspiracy?' she asked.

'Well,' said Clay, 'that, of course, brings in the questions of accessories and murder in the second degree. It depends largely how it's looked on by the judge and jury. I wouldn't answer offhand. But now about this robbery — you say you and Vintner planned it?'

'Yes. I had been embezzling money for years,' said Miss Martin calmly. 'I had always covered it from other deposits.

Discovery was at last imminent, and I had become desperate from fear. The plan was to have Vintner rob the safe in the early evening when the Fothergill Street door was likely to be unfastened. Then we were to divide the proceeds.'

'I understood you to say,' said Clay, 'that you *never* touched a penny of the proceeds?'

'I was referring to the theft of goods from the stockroom, which had been going on for years. Mr. Timson stole heavily. Mr. Embrich was an old man, and had some heart trouble which made it unlikely that he would live long. I had saved nothing, and his death would very likely mean the loss of my position. If Mr. Timson could make thousands, why shouldn't I?'

'When you discovered these thefts, you never thought of goin' to Mr. Embrich about it?'

'Never. You see, I didn't discover what was going on until the thefts had become so enormous that I should probably have been dismissed myself for dereliction of duty. So I decided to follow suit. I arranged with Vintner for the crime to be committed on an evening when I thought Mr. Embrich would not be at the office. When I found he was staying late, it was too late to change the plans. I went home. Next morning Mr. Embrich was found murdered, and the contents of the safe were gone. There's no going beyond that.'

'And how about that handkerchief?'

'That was an afterthought. I got down next morning before anyone arrived. I knew Mann opened the side door at half past seven and then went to the front of the store. When I saw Mr. Embrich dead, and the blood on the floor, I was more overcome than I had expected to be. Then I saw a handkerchief of Jenny Friend's on Mr. Embrich's desk. She was always leaving hers about, and must have put it there when she was taking dictation. I hated Jenny, because I was afraid Mr. Embrich meant someday to give her my position. I saw the chance to incriminate her, knowing she went with Vintner. I scrubbed the floor with it and stuffed it down the drain. Then I went out and came back at my usual time. Nobody had seen me.'

She stopped. Clay sat fingering his mustache. He looked up and shook his head. 'I can't make head or tail of all this *lyin*',' he said. 'Course, you're crazy about young Goodloe, and want to get him free. But that tale wouldn't fool a green cop. Sounds like an overnight resolve mixed with a dream.'

'One part's true, Mr. Clay,' Rosanna interposed. 'I saw Miss Martin scrub the floor with the handkerchief, but it was at night. With your permission, I'll tell you what occurred. I did telephone to Mr. Embrich's house, as Peck rightly told you. When he informed me that my uncle was working late, I resolved to go down and see him. It was an impulse, but I felt that I had acted wrongly in keeping away from him, and I wanted to tell him that I was sorry. I couldn't forget how kind he had always been to me.

'I reached the store at about half past ten, going in by the Fothergill Street door, which was unlocked and partly open. I went up the stairs and into Miss Martin's room. The inner door was ajar. The first thing I saw was Philip, standing in the middle of the room — '

'The damn skunk!' shouted Jones. 'He said Rosanna got there *first*, and that he found *her* there. You heard him, Clay! He *lied*, the hound, to put another inch of safety between himself and the chair!'

Rosanna shot a quick glance at Jones, and continued, 'Then I saw Mr. Embrich's body huddled up in the chair. I screamed; my uncle was stone dead. I don't know what I did then.'

Clay's face was stolid, enigmatical, expressionless. The inspector was hanging on every movement of Rosanna's lips.

'When I became calmer I taxed Philip with killing him. He swore that he had not. He said that he had come to the store to talk to him about something that he had said to him that afternoon, on the occasion of their quarrel — something about his getting out and going to work. He swore he had only been there a minute when I came in, and had found him dead.

'I believed him. We talked it over. I wanted to notify the police instantly. But Philip was afraid. He said we should both be arrested, that he would certainly go to the chair as my uncle's murderer, and I would get a life sentence. Still I didn't want to leave it like that. It was too ghastly. But when Philip insisted, I — well, I gave way.

'He was so grateful. He kissed me — ' Jones scowled. ' — and went home at once. I followed him out of the room. I was so unnerved I didn't know what to do. It seemed like a horrible nightmare to me. I couldn't make myself believe that Uncle Cy was really dead. I went back and looked at him again.

'At last I realized that for Philip's sake I must go away unseen. I had just got as far as the head of the stairs when I heard someone coming up. I shrank back against the wall, as close as I could get. It was Miss Martin. She didn't notice me.

'She went into her room. Then I heard her cry out. After that came a long silence. I heard a faint scrubbing sound coming from my uncle's office. I stole to the door and looked in. I saw Miss Martin on her hands and knees, scouring the blood from the floor with a handkerchief.

'I had just time to get back to the end of the passage when Miss Martin came out again, reeling and muttering. I thought she was demented. When she went down the stairs, I followed, and watched her from the door of Mr. Clark's room. But she never noticed me. She was holding the handkerchief in her hand. I saw quite clearly the initial F upon it.

'Miss Martin wandered about the yard, as if she did not know what she was doing. There was nobody there. Mann was not there. He did not seem to be on duty that night. I saw Miss Martin lift the handkerchief by the corner several times, as if she was about to put it down somewhere, and then change her mind.

'At last she stopped before the drainpipe. She hesitated a moment or two, and then thrust the handkerchief down it. Then she came back, walked past me and out into the street, and still never saw me. I went into the street after her. I still meant to accost her, but she was walking quickly away, and I recalled my promise to Philip. So I went home. That's all that happened that night, so far as I know.'

Miss Martin turned a somber gaze upon the girl, sitting motionless in her chair. Clay did not relax a muscle of his face. Adelaide, leaning over the chair in which Rosanna sat, laid a hand caressingly upon the girl's shoulder.

'It wasn't true that Jenny was in training for Miss Martin's job,' continued Rosanna, showing signs of breaking down for the first time. 'But it was clear that Miss Martin did wish it to be believed that Jenny had been implicated in the murder, and that the girl had therefore some connection with it, if she had not actually stabbed my uncle.

'Then I got to thinking, and wondering, why, if it was part of Miss Martin's purpose to throw the guilt on Jenny, she hadn't bought a handkerchief with the initial J — standing for Jenny's first name. And then it was that the idea of a possible explanation came to me, and I realized, also, that Miss Martin had left no stone unturned in her scheme to have my uncle die.

'Mr. Clay, when I asked you to show me that handkerchief, I was looking for a tiny irregularity in the threads of the weave, a sort of *stretching* just where the lowest cross-stroke of the E would have been if the initial had been an E instead of an F. And I found what I was looking for.

'Miss Martin didn't buy that handkerchief. She used one of her own, but she pulled out the threads of the embroidery that constituted the lowest cross-stroke of the E, thus making an F out of it. Look at it under your glass, Mr. Clay, and notice it. Observe also that the thread has been snipped off smooth with scissors, instead of being frayed.'

Miss Martin cried out, gasped, and sat in her chair, rigid as a cataleptic, staring at Rosanna. For the first time Clay's impassivity seemed to abandon him. He looked quickly from one woman to the other, almost as astounded as that day in the store when Rosanna asked him her memorable question.

Rosanna turned to Miss Martin. 'Tell Inspector Clay the whole truth,' she said, 'about your motive and about everything, or else I'll have to. It will sound better from your lips than mine. If you wish to save Philip from the chair, tell all you know — *all of it!*'

The rigid figure in the chair collapsed. A moan broke from Miss Martin's lips. 'Yes, I will — I will tell everything,' Miss Martin answered.

Huddled up, her hands gripped each other, and the fingers intertwining restlessly, the secretary said, 'I'm Philip Goodloe's mother. I married his father, Henry Goodloe, Cyrus Embrich's half-brother, years ago in Kansas City. He neglected me, and I became infatuated with another man, and ran away, leaving the baby behind.

'That madness only lasted a month. I wrote my husband, imploring his forgiveness, for the sake of the child. I received a letter from his lawyer, saying that Mr. Goodloe refused. Divorce proceedings, he added, had been instituted.

'Henry Goodloe divorced me. Soon afterward he killed himself, but I was not the cause of his death. He shot himself. He had lost everything in an oil smash. Cyrus Embrich took care of Philip in New York. I had never met Cyrus, but I had once written to him, imploring him to intercede for me with Henry, and my letters had come back to me without a word of answer. I knew how strong the family affection between the brothers was, and that Cyrus Embrich would never recognize me, never permit me to see the child. But their affection was no stronger than my love for Philip. I resolved to devote the rest of my life to watching over my boy, even if, as has happened, he never knew me.

'I came East and got a position in Cyrus Embrich's store as saleslady. I was soon taken out of the sales department and transferred to the office. It was easy for me, too, to secure my standing with Mr. Embrich. I was good-looking then, and a good-looking woman could *always* obtain an influence over him. In a short time I became his secretary; he trusted me more and more, until he left me practically to run the business. And, by humoring his weaknesses, I reached the point where I became indispensable.

'In fact, I could have married him. But that was not my aim. My one thought was to watch over my son. I could hardly conceal my emotion the first time I saw him again, then a boy of 7 years. And all these years I have been watching over him, and keeping him and his uncle on good terms.'

She was shaking with emotion now, and the words fell from her lips in a torrent of burning speech.

'They say there is a nemesis that waits for all who have fallen by the wayside. Sooner or later, I had known, the truth must be discovered. And my nemesis appeared in Peck.

'It is extraordinary that in a nation of more than a hundred million people, two should meet twice by chance, at intervals of many thousand miles. But this is constantly happening, and therefore I felt no surprise when Peck, who was down on his luck, and had happened to obtain some temporary work in the addressing department, encountered me one day. He had been our chauffeur — Henry Goodloe's and mine — for a month or two after our marriage.

'He was quite frank with me. He

demanded the payment of several hundred dollars as the price of his silence, promising to return to the West and never trouble me again. I paid him four hundred and fifty, all I had in the world. I only hoped for a respite. Every day that I could see my son growing up was so much gain to me, and by this time I was constantly at Mr. Embrich's house. Philip liked me in those early days.'

There was a sobbing in the room, but it came from Adelaide, not from Miss Martin.

'Six months later I had a letter from Peck, demanding five hundred more. I paid no attention to it. Two months later he came to the office, threatened me, and — I paid.

'That gave me a short respite only. But Peck realized I had no more money, and about this time made the acquaintance of Mr. Timson, my assistant; the end of it was that the two began a system of steady blackmail. Using Vintner, who, however, I believe, was not informed of my story, they compelled me to assist with a systematic robbery of the store, which went on for years.

'Timson needed money to enable him to keep up his manner of life. In some way he seemed to have a hold over Mr. Embrich, though I never knew how. These two men, and their tool, kept me in a condition of desperation. Only Mr. Embrich's old-fashioned methods enabled me to prevent him from discovering what was going on. And, as I said, I never received a penny of the proceeds. They knew my love for Philip, and traded on it to the full.

'Rosanna Beach was the third person who knew. I confided in her one day, when I was desperate. That was the reason why she left Mr. Embrich's house.'

Rosanna looked up at Clay, and nodded her assent.

'Two or three weeks ago,' Miss Martin continued, 'discovery appeared imminent. Mr. Embrich could not understand why the receipts had fallen off so. He spoke of a thorough auditing, which, of course, would have uncovered the ingenious system of fraud that Timson and I had hammered out. But by this time I had become reckless enough not to care. Something new had transpired: Mr. Embrich was threatening to disinherit Philip — my son — on account of Miss Beach. Perhaps my moral sense had atrophied, but I resolved that, come what might, Philip should inherit his share of his uncle's money.

'I laid my plans with greatest care. I spoke of the imminent discovery of the robberies. Timson and I agreed that the game had been played out. One coup, the greatest of all, and then it must be each for himself. The very day, the last possible day, was selected.

'I was to arrange to place certain securities and moneys in the safe in Mr. Embrich's office, and leave it open. I knew the combination, but some spark of loyalty — perverted, of course — to Mr. Embrich prevented my revealing it. The other course was as good; Mr. Embrich, even if he were at the office, would not go to the safe. You see, I knew him like a book.'

'You didn't place them there,' said Jones. 'You told them that last night.'

'I did *not*,' answered the secretary, 'nor did I ever have any intention of doing so.

I had paid enough to those blackmailers. My plan was a deeper one. The subject which they had discussed as a possibility, I meant to make the entire purpose.

'I resolved that Vintner should murder Mr. Embrich.

'I knew the old man was full of courage, and would certainly tackle any intruder. I led him, by suggestions during the week before, to arrange to stay nightly in his office, under the plea that no one but himself could properly understand the fluctuations in market prices. Of course, I did not tell the others of this.

'Then I talked with Vintner, who had come out of jail raging because he had been made the sole victim. I told him that the discovery of the thefts, which had been made by one of Mr. Clark's men, had been limited, through my agency, so that the extent of the scheme was undreamed of. I told him he might have had twenty years instead of six months, but for me.

'I inflamed his mind against Mr. Embrich, telling him that Jenny Friend had been at his house, and insinuating that he was unduly interested in the girl. I got him into a condition where a chance encounter with Mr. Embrich in his office would result in murder.

'I was desperate enough to view everything with the coolest detachment. I felt that he deserved to die, I think, if I thought it at all, but my solicitude for Philip outweighed every consideration of morality. Poor boy, he had never *learned* to work!

'My plan was for Vintner to murder Mr. Embrich, and to be trapped, while the others would thus be implicated as well. I did not care what happened to me. I should have a day's start in my flight from the law, and I was accustomed to being an outcast and a fugitive. And Philip would be saved from being disinherited.

'As it turns out, it was all useless, for Mr. Embrich was already married — I am assuming that the marriage is proved — and his will was already in existence.

'It was only Philip's arrest the next morning which, coming as a stunning and unlooked-for blow, held me in New York and changed my plans.

271

'Then, after Vintner was arrested, I expected him to denounce me every moment. I never slept. How he put up that plea I cannot understand, but I suppose the doctors erred in some way, and that Vintner committed the murder before being arrested in Central Park.

'I was resolved that Vintner should not escape. I arranged to call in Mr. Jones as soon as the murder was discovered, because he had been instrumental in the former arrest of Vintner for the robberies, and I knew that his mind would therefore insensibly be prejudiced in favor of Vintner as the murderer.

'For the same reason I told Mr. Clark that I had seen Vintner in the yard that afternoon. It was not true, but I knew that it would be remembered.

'In order to make the evidence more cumulative, it was necessary to implicate Jenny Friend, who had been going with Vintner. With that idea in mind, I did exactly what Miss Beach detected. I picked out the thread of the tail of the initial E upon my handkerchief, meaning to leave the handkerchief somewhere near the body in the morning.

'But after the time fixed for the murder had gone I became too agitated to be able to remain at home. I had to know whether or not Vintner had killed Mr. Embrich. I went down to the store and saw Mr. Embrich lying dead. It was then I thought of the plan of scrubbing the floor with the handkerchief, which afterward I stuffed down the drainpipe.

'I had no regrets, and I have none now. I hated Jenny Friend because she was in a way implicated in the sequence of events which led up to the disinheriting of my son.

'I should have remained in New York until Philip was released. But when the story of his confession came out I grew frantic. I went to Timson and told him the truth must be revealed, no matter what the cost. He sent Peck to me with a message to meet them all at that haunt on Eleventh Avenue last night.

'Mr. Jones here can tell you what happened, though I don't know how he got on the trail. Vintner had the audacity to deny that he murdered Mr. Embrich. I defied them, and they tried to murder me. I called the police.

'I'm ready to go to the chair for my part in the murder. But I tell you, as surely as I sit here, by the motherhood of women, that I have come because my son is innocent and Vintner is guilty!'

She ceased speaking and huddled up again, her sharp eyes fixed pathetically on Clay's face. Clay was biting the ends of his mustache. The women sobbed openly. It was a full minute before Clay broke the silence.

'How about those lilies, Miss Martin?' he inquired. 'What was it they were meant to signify?'

'I know nothing about them,' the secretary answered.

'They weren't there when you went home?'

'No, certainly not! Mr. Embrich never would have flowers on his desk, or in any of the offices.'

'Somebody must have brought 'em there,' continued Clay, glancing up at Rosanna, who shook her head.

Clay rose. 'Very good; I'm glad to have

heard you ladies,' he said. 'And, Miss Beach, I'm goin' to take you in under the warrant that's been issued for you. Charge: murder of Cyrus Embrich.'

Miss Martin leaped to her feet, her whole body vibrating, as if on wires. 'You — don't — believe — what I've been telling you, Inspector Clay?' she gasped.

Rosanna interposed: 'It makes no difference whether Mr. Clay believes it or not. Neither Vintner nor you had any hand in Mr. Embrich's murder.'

'Holy Smoke!' exclaimed Clay, startled into the expletive. 'Well, Miss Beach, ain't those the lines I'm proceedin' on?'

'Yes,' said Rosanna, 'but I didn't kill my uncle, either. And neither did Philip. Now, Mr. Clay, will you listen to me one moment?'

'Ah, what's the use?' growled Clay. 'We've traveled straight round the mulberry bush back to the startin' point nine times already.'

'Suppose I could get a confession from the actual murderer?'

Clay threw up his hands. 'There's been too much confessin' — *squealin'*, some'd call it,' he objected.

'I can show you the murderer, and probably obtain a confession, if you'll have me taken to Mrs. Embrich's apartment at about nine o'clock tonight, and come yourself, and . . . wait.'

'And you say you'll show me another murderer for sure?'

'The one and only person who killed my uncle.'

'Got it all fixed so's he'll turn up for sure on time?' demanded Clay.

'Exactly,' answered Rosanna.

'And how'll I know who's speakin' the truth then?' asked Clay.

'You'll know,' replied Rosanna.

'You're on,' said Clay, after a moment's reflection.

15

Whether or not Clay actually believed Rosanna guilty, it is certain that he took no precautions on the way to Adelaide's apartment that night to prevent her from being rescued by anyone who might be lying in wait with that object in view.

Arriving at the apartment, they rang Adelaide's bell, pushed open the door without waiting for the click, and climbed the long flights of stairs. To Clay's surprise, when Jones and the actress appeared at the door of her flat, it could be seen that the interior was absolutely dark.

'Rosanna!' exclaimed Adelaide, embracing the girl. 'Come in, Inspector Clay!' she added. 'Turn into that door and sit down on the lounge that you'll feel on the right-hand side.'

Clay obeyed; he even let Rosanna go during the process. But when they were all seated, he growled, 'The boys at the bureau would say I was the nuttiest cop who ever joined the force, if they could see me with a desperate young female criminal, trustin' myself in a dark room like this.'

'Mr. Clay,' said Adelaide, 'I know you don't believe Miss Beach is guilty.'

'I never did,' Clay growled in his throat.

'Well, what about — ' began Jones in surprise.

Clay waved an invisible hand at him. 'Forget it, Mr. Jones!' he answered. 'I said the evidence pointed to her and Mr. Goodloe as bein' the authors of Mr. Embrich's murder. I didn't say I believed the evidence, did I? There's no opinions to my job; it's just followin' up the clues.'

'Then who do you think — ' Jones began again.

Clay ran an invisible finger round the line of his collar. 'You can search me,' he answered. 'It's got me guessin'. I guess I've been guessin' since the beginnin'. Show me some fresh light on the subject, and I'll strike off on a new trail. Till that light comes, I'll follow the old one. But say,' he added, 'talkin' of lights, what's the idea of sittin' here in the dark? If it's any

278

spiritualist business — ' He drew a long breath. ' — I never fell for it yet, and in the line of my duty, no!'

'It's not spiritualism, Mr. Clay,' said Adelaide. 'We're waiting for a burglar.'

Clay grunted. 'Mighty obligin' burglar to notify you of the hour of his arrival, I must say!' he soliloquized.

'That burglar,' said Rosanna, 'is the person who killed Mr. Embrich.'

'Got any proof?'

'He'll probably confess. If he doesn't, you'll see the guilt on his face. Anyway, I promise you it won't take you long to make up your mind.'

'Well, I'm willin' to be shown,' said the inspector. 'By the way, Mrs. Embrich, there was a large cut of yourself in one of them theatrical papers this morning, sayin' that you'd left for the South this mornin' with a tourin' company. Some of the boys at the bureau showed it to me. Guess they got you doped wrong?'

'It looks like it,' answered Adelaide. 'But now I'm just going to strike a match to show you your bearings.'

She struck one, shielding the little

flame with her hand, so as to conceal it from any possible observation through the window of the room opposite. 'This is the living room,' she said. 'You see my bedroom behind those curtains, which I've drawn back. That's the bathroom across the hall.

'Now our burglar will certainly sound the bell to make sure that I'm at home. You see, he's an early bird, and carries out all his operations well before midnight. When the bell rings, we go through the bathroom window and conceal ourselves on the fire escape.

'There's no likelihood of his going into the bathroom, and as soon as he's busy at work in the bedroom and living room we'll climb back into the bathroom and watch him through the holes which I've made in the door. Then, when I give the signal, it will be up to you to arrest him, Mr. Clay.'

'And you give me your word,' asked Clay, 'that this arrest is goin' to solve the Embrich mystery?'

'I do,' said both women together.

'All right,' said Clay. 'I'll take you at your word, ladies. But that confession'll have to come out good and strong and convincin'.'

As he spoke the bell of the street door buzzed. Adelaide rose and led the way into the bathroom opposite. The party followed her silently, clambered out of the open window, and took up their positions on the fire escape outside.

Presently, the door opened. A finger of light from a flashlight traveled uncannily along the hall. Then, by its reflection backward, they could discern the wizened figure of a little old man. He was dressed in a workman's overalls and wore a long, loose overcoat which hung open beneath a coarse, heavy muffler that covered the lower part of the face. A slouch hat on the head was pressed down to the eyebrows.

Anything less like a professional burglar it was impossible to imagine; the man looked like an old tramp, and only his business-like way of procedure indicated that he was anything but a novice at the game. And that was probably due to the fact that he had been in the flat before.

He passed straight into Adelaide's bed-room. The watchers, having re-entered the bathroom softly and neatly closed the door, kept their eyes glued to the four round holes which had been bored, some distance apart, in the woodwork.

By the light he carried, the intruder could be seen tossing over the contents of Adelaide's desk. Bundles of letters, tied up with ribbon, were carefully inspected.

Apparently the burglar was looking for the postmarks of those of recent date, for he rejected nearly all of these, scattering them about the floor; and confining his attention to a few loose letters which he extracted from their envelopes, he sat down upon the floor to read them by the light. A quarter of an hour must have passed before, having apparently satisfied his curiosity, he threw the letters upon the desk and proceeded to open the door of the closet in which Adelaide's clothes were hanging. With extraordinary celerity, he tore the garments from their hooks and proceeded to hold up each one and examine it.

'That's too bad, Adelaide!' Jones heard Rosanna whisper very softly, as the girl stood with set teeth at the sight of this vandalism.

But there was worse to come. Apparently the burglar was of an extremely Puritanical disposition, for, while he critically surveyed the plainer garments, the more elaborate ones came in for much harsher treatment.

Holding up a diaphanous, abbreviated frock, he inspected it, fingered it, clicked his teeth, shook his head viciously, and, with low mutterings, flung it in a crumpled mass across the room toward the radiator, where it caught and hung by one sleeve.

Having at length completed a minute examination of Adelaide's clothing, the burglar turned his attention to the chest of drawers. He began tossing out quantities of clothing and, squatting upon the floor, continued his examination with these.

Something white and edged with filmy lace came in for savage disapproval. With a fierce grunt, the intruder took it in his two hands and ripped it from end to end, tossing it beneath the bed.

At her observation point, Adelaide was straining like a dog on a leash. Jones felt Rosanna's hand cross his and grip the girl's hard. Clay turned his bullet-head toward the two women.

'Some burglar!' he commented in the throatiest of whispers. 'Whenever ya say the word, I'm ready, ladies!'

But nobody stirred. The burglar, having ransacked the drawers, began to investigate the toilet articles upon the dressing-table. Bottles of lotion were picked up and set down; an ivory brush was thrown into a corner; an ivory powder-box was emptied of its contents, which lay in a pale pink pyramid upon the floor. Finally the intruder swept the whole upon the bed, where the fluids from the broken bottles mingled in a vast, spreading, vari-colored stain.

Still Adelaide remained silent. But there was something curious in her pose; she looked as if she had been suddenly frozen or petrified. Jones heard her gasp, '*Rosanna!*'

'Hmm?'

'Is it — is it . . . you let me think that it was Timson's *wife!*'

'I had to! I wasn't sure! Not dead sure! How could I tell you, Adelaide, before I knew? It had to be gone through just the same!'

Adelaide Embrich shook her off fiercely. 'My God!' she moaned, and suddenly collapsed, a silent heap upon the floor at Jones's feet.

Meanwhile the burglar, who had been examining the knickknacks on the walls, had picked up the photograph of Mr. Embrich and, with an unexpected gesture, pressed it to his lips. At the sound of Adelaide's cry, however, he started. A look of awful fear flashed over his face.

And then Clay leaped into the room, and Jones followed him.

Instantly the burglar was transformed into a spitting, flying fury. He hurled the flashlight into Jones's face. There might have been a wildcat in the apartment. The elusive body seemed all fire and springs. It writhed and fought and struggled and clutched in the two men's hands, combating with feet and nails and teeth, and the growls that came from its throat were mingled with imprecations and blasphemous prayers.

'Switch on the light!' Inspector Clay

was shouting. 'Kneel on him, Jones! I've got him!'

As the light flashed on, the figure suddenly collapsed upon the floor and lay quiescent. Jones saw Rosanna supporting the unconscious body of Adelaide Embrich in the bathroom. He looked down at the intruder's face, grown suddenly resigned. The hat had fallen off, the muffler lay upon the floor, and the face revealed was that of an old woman — of Mrs. Mann.

The absurd figure had become a tragic one. It was absurdly, horridly incongruous with its gray hair and placid, motherly face, now showing no trace of the former frenzy.

Inspector Clay gave the old woman his arm and led her to an armchair. She took her seat in it and looked at him as a mother on a child.

Suddenly Adelaide Embrich came tottering through the doorway and sank down at the old woman's knees. *'Mother!'* she wept.

Mrs. Mann's hands crept out and stroked Adelaide's hair. 'We're *all* sinners!' she said. 'God forbid that *I* should judge!'

'Mother, tell them you didn't — didn't — kill — '

'Aye, but I killed,' she answered. 'I killed Cyrus that night because I loved him. He was so good. He was the best man that effer lived. He was father to us, and we were his children. God knoweth how I wrastled with your father, after he drove you from his house, to become the Scarlet Woman of Babylon. God knoweth a father should not drive his daughter forth because she has committed the sin, taken the false step that leadeth to perdition.

'Had you no home, that you should have gone after such abominations, become a play-actress in the accursed pictures? When you came home and told your father that, his wrath flared up. I was a reed in his hands. I strove with him vainly.

'But a mother neffer forgets. I wrastled with the Lord for you. At last He spoke to me. 'Go forth,' He said, 'find her and learn what sins she doeth.' And so I went forth nightly, walking the streets of the evil city, up and down — yes, I walked in the street of the theaters and other abominations; but it was long before I found you.

'At last the day came when I saw you, child, and followed you to your home. Then I returned and told your father. All night long we wrastled, one with another, in groanings and prayers. And at last the message came to us that fire must be fought with fire.

'So I learned all the evil of the theaters, and I bought me papers of actresses, and portraits on every page. Often I have seen your portrait staring out at me from one of them. In this way I could follow you in the spirit. In this way I learned where you had gone to spread sin among the people of other cities.

'When you were gone I went to the flat in which you lived. It was my task to learn what evil you were committing, because you were my child. And thus I learned and, when you came back, I watched nightly across the street, and I knew that men called to visit you in the evenings.

'It became my task to warn them that they were endangering their souls. But when I looked them in the face, and saw the stamp of Hell upon them, I held back. For evil seeketh evil, and these men were neffer of the elect.

'Then came the day when I saw Mr. Embrich leave your home, and I knew that your evil had entrapped the best man that effer lived. After that I kept watch more closely. And, as he came night by night, I knew that Satan had bound you to him, and that each day his soul decayed and dwindled, till soon he would be plucked bodily forth and cast into hell. And then it was the message came to me: 'GO FORTH, PUT THINE HAND TO THE KNIFE; DELAY NOT; STRIKE AND SLAY; FOR SO SHALT THOU DELIVER HIS SOUL ALIVE!'

'But of this I said nothing to Mann, for he was sorely troubled, and all his nights he spent in wrastlings and prayers. So I went forth upon my errand.

'Yet, first, being unwilling to do that which was laid upon me, I went to your flat again. I entered your flat, and saw the photograph of Mr. Embrich. I read your letters. I learned that you had ensnared his heart. He profaned the name of wife to call you thereby. Yet I went away, and again all night I wrastled.

'The next night I went again. Upon the table lay a box with the name of another man thereupon. I opened it. It was filled with flowers. And then my heart was filled with jealous anger and eagerness to fulfill the message. I took two flowers, and hesitated no more, but went down to the store, meaning to hide there in Mr. Embrich's office until he came in the morning, and do the slaying then.

'When I reached there, I looked into Mann's shanty, and saw him upon his knees asleep. He had slept while wrastling, from weariness of the spirit. Then I knew my message was true, and nought could make me fail. So I went softly up the stairs toward the office, where I had been before when Mr. Embrich summoned me to wish me a merry Christmas and to give me a goose and a suit for Bobby.

'I went into the next room. I tried Mr. Embrich's door softly. It did not yield. I placed my little key in the lock and opened it. He sat there in his chair, fast sleeping. Even then I drew back. Hiss face was so kind! Not yet had Satan stolen his soul from him, for the wicked sleep not.

'And then, upon the table, I saw the sign — the sharp, thin knife with the razor's edge, set there for my own hand. I hesitated no more. I drove the blade deep into his body with all my strength.

'He stirred and moaned, opened his eyes, and looked at me. His hand moved on the table. 'Tis God, not I, strikes you down, to save your soul from Hell, dear master,' I said to him. 'He hath chosen me to be His handmaid and His instrument.' He nodded and fell asleep. So I went home.

'But first I laid the lilies upon the desk in front of him in token of the divine forgiveness. God rest his soul. He was the best man who effer lived.'

She ceased speaking and shuddered; then a look of benign, compassionate forgiveness came upon her face as she drew the weeping girl's head down to her knee.

Clay rose again and gave Mrs. Mann his arm. Leaning on it, she let him lead her from the room.

'And so,' said Clay, a few days later in his office, 'the Embrich mystery didn't happen to be so much of a mystery. I guess there is somethin' in that system of yours, Mr. Jones. You said a woman did it, and a woman did, and you said a man nearly did it, and a man nearly did. But I can't see how it got anywhere, without the practical cooperation.

'But, what puzzles me,' continued Clay, turning also toward the girl, 'is how you arranged to have that poor crazed woman burgle Mrs. Embrich's apartment just when you wanted her to.'

'Well, that wasn't so hard,' Rosanna answered. 'You see, I got that fake news into the theatrical paper saying that she'd gone South, and I knew her mother would spot it and get on the job right away.'

'But how'd ya guess who she was — or, anyways, that the Manns were interested in theatrical doin's?' asked the inspector.

'Well,' said Rosanna, 'it all hangs on a very simple point. You remember that morning in the store — when you upset the pail of water over my dress?' Clay cleared his throat gruffly and nodded. 'I'd picked up something, too. I thought it wouldn't do much good to disclose it then. You didn't go inside the watchman's shanty.'

'I guess I didn't,' Clay admitted.

'I did. I saw a torn copy of a theatrical paper lying under his bench. I picked it up and saw that it was dog-eared at the page with Adelaide's photograph. Then I saw a crumpled ball of paper, and I picked that up and saw another photograph of her upon it. So, when I came out, I asked you if Mann was a sporting character, and you told me he was a street preacher.

'I thought something was queer, and when you took us to the Mann house I slipped inside and looked about. When I came upon a heap of torn pages from the theatrical papers, with Adelaide's photograph in them, I saw at once that Adelaide was in all probability Mann's daughter.

'When I left you, Mr. Jones,' Rosanna continued, 'I needed only that point cleared up in order to have a working hypothesis. I was pretty sure Miss Martin wouldn't have murdered Mr. Embrich and then gone back to look at his body an hour later. I suppose you didn't notice that little photograph on the wall of Adelaide's living-room?'

'No, I — ' said Jones.

'But I recognized it at once as that of Mann and his wife. Moreover, it was taken in Cardiff, many years ago. So my quest was already at an end.

'I went to Adelaide and begged her to hide me. I didn't — couldn't tell her that I suspected her own father and mother. I wasn't sure which it was until the actual burglary. I let her infer that I suspected Mrs. Timson.

'I discovered within an hour that Bobby Mann had known all along of his sister's whereabouts. Then, having no need to investigate Sanford Rogers further, I put Bobby on you, to trail you, and warn me if you went into danger.

'That's about all,' Rosanna concluded. 'I reached the Manns by the simple process of elimination. Of course, I was afraid, horribly afraid, that I had been all wrong. But my intuition — well, I guess there really was something in what you said about *that*.'

Jones nodded glumly. Clay was staring at Rosanna dumbly. Twice he tried to speak, then shook his head and burst out: 'All I can say, Miss Beach, is anytime you're thinkin' of makin' a change, there'll be an empty chair for you on the detective force. But I guess you wouldn't leave Jones.'

'No, I'm going to keep at work right up to the week I'm married,' Rosanna answered.

16

'You see, Miss Beach,' expounded Jones in his office a week afterward, 'the system's just what I always claimed it was, but it needs practical application, and that's the element that I'm unable to bring to it. And now you're leaving me, I don't suppose I'll ever get the right sort of cooperation.'

'Um!' said Rosanna. 'What makes you talk about me leaving you, Mr. Jones? Going to fire me?'

'Not on your life, Miss Beach! But I can't imagine that you'll have the need to come back to work after you're married.'

'I wonder!' said Rosanna thoughtfully, and she put her left hand on her lap.

'You see,' said Jones, 'both Mr. Goodloe and you are fairly comfortably off, or will be, when the will's probated.'

'Mr. Goodloe?' asked the girl. 'Yes, but — but what makes you mention Philip in connection with my position here?'

'Er — not with your position here, Miss Beach, except indirectly,' answered Jones. 'I was thinking of him in connection with — er — your marrying, I mean.'

'You mean you wish me to marry Philip?' inquired Rosanna.

'Why — er — yes,' said Jones stoutly. 'At least, I understood — '

'Well, I won't!' snapped Rosanna, looking at him with very bright eyes. 'Do you suppose,' she went on, 'that I — I'd marry a man who — who tried to save his skin by *lying* about the woman he was engaged to?'

Jones, very deeply moved, swung round in his swivel-chair. He took Rosanna's left hand in his enormous left, and patted it with the other.

'I — er — Miss Beach, I'm so much older than you that I — er — experience of life, you know. I'm sure that Mr. Goodloe did not *mean* to inculpate you with that statement. Remember the fearful strain the man was under.'

'He skulked behind a woman's skirt to save his miserable life!' cried Rosanna.

'We all do that,' said Jones. 'If you

reject Mr. Goodloe after your — your
common comradeship in danger, you'll
— er — may be sorry, you know.'

And he swung round abruptly, and,
taking up a pen, began drawing furiously
upon a sheet of paper.

Dead silence. Rosanna winked away a
tear or two. A very tender smile came on
her face. She got up softly and went to
Jones's side. She looked over his shoulder.

'Mr. Jones!' said Rosanna. 'Stop it!
Stop that nonsense of yours. There are
more important things to be done.'

Jones laid down his pen obediently,
looked up, and pushed the red mane out
of his eyes.

'Mr. Jones, you're the very worst,
blindest, stupidest detective in the whole
world!'

'Well — I believe I am,' said Jones.

Rosanna laid her left hand flat down on
the sheet of paper. 'And *you* can't *see*
things immediately before your eyes,' she
said.

Jones looked at the hand. 'Why, you're
not wearing — ' he began. He looked at
Rosanna's face, and a slow dawning

comprehension began to come upon his own.

He took her hand in his. 'Miss B — Rosanna,' he said, 'the laws of probability show that after the first and second times of asking in marriage the chance of subsequent acceptance falls to — in short — it's only that — that — Rosanna! Will you marry me? Won't — *will you?*'

'I think I ought to,' said Rosanna; and then, slyly, '*after* you add *my* name to the glass on your door.'

THE END

We do hope that you have enjoyed reading this large print book.

Did you know that all of our titles are available for purchase?

We publish a wide range of high quality large print books including:
Romances, Mysteries, Classics
General Fiction
Non Fiction and Westerns

Special interest titles available in large print are:
The Little Oxford Dictionary
Music Book, Song Book
Hymn Book, Service Book

Also available from us courtesy of Oxford University Press:
Young Readers' Dictionary
(large print edition)
Young Readers' Thesaurus
(large print edition)

For further information or a free brochure, please contact us at:
Ulverscroft Large Print Books Ltd.,
The Green, Bradgate Road, Anstey,
Leicester, LE7 7FU, England.
Tel: (00 44) **0116 236 4325**
Fax: (00 44) **0116 234 0205**

Other titles in the
Linford Mystery Library:

THE SILVER HORSESHOE

Gerald Verner

John Arbinger receives an anonymous note — offering 'protection' from criminal gangs in exchange for £5,000 — with the impression of a tiny silver horseshoe in the bottom right-hand corner. Ignoring the author's warning about going to the police, Arbinger seeks the help of Superintendent Budd of Scotland Yard. But Budd is too late to save Arbinger from the deadly consequences of his actions, and soon the activities of the Silver Horseshoe threaten the public at large — as well as the lives of Budd and his stalwart companions . . .

A MURDER MOST MACABRE

Edmund Glasby

Jeremy Lavelle, leader of the esoteric Egyptian Society the Order of the True Sphinx, has illegally purchased an ancient Egyptian mummy. Watched by his enthralled followers, he opens the coffin and begins to unwrap the body . . . The head is that of an ancient scribe, his shrivelled and desiccated face staring eyelessly up from his coffin — yet from the neck down, wrapped up in layers of bandages, are not the mummified remains which they had expected. Instead, they stare in horror at the decapitated corpse of a recently killed man!

NEMESIS

Norman Firth

A burlesque beauty's fierce yearning for vengeance is triggered following the callous shooting of her younger sister in a gang war. Rita's single-handed efforts to avenge her sister's death bring her into contact with some of gangland's most ruthless killers, whose animal instincts cause them to treat life cheaply, and women callously. Through many dangers Rita pursues her determined way towards the clearing of the mystery surrounding her sister's slaying, and the vengeance which has set her whole being aflame . . .

BLOOD MOON

V. J. Banis

Jeannie feels the aggressive grimness of the Atlantic island even before her boat lands. Under the assumed identity of governess to young Varda, she has come to Langdon's Purlieu to investigate the mysterious death of her half-sister, the child's mother. Once in the house, she cannot understand why the servants seem perpetually frightened. 'Please, miss!' the maid begs her. 'Leave this place! Leave before the blood moon rises over the sea!' Can Jeannie unravel the secrets of the old house, or will she die in the attempt?

MURDERS GALORE

Richard A. Lupoff

Murders Galore is a collection of six stories that range through time and place from a World War Two military post, to a Midwestern industrial city, to a boys' vacation camp, to a transcontinental streamliner. The macabre methods and motives involved are as varied as the venues, but the result in each case is — *murder!* Beginning with *The Square Root of Dead*, in which a doomed mathematics professor devises, in his final moments, an ingenious way to identify his killer . . .

THE TUDOR GARDEN MYSTERY

Gerald Verner

When one of Sir Richard Alperton's house guests is murdered in the Tudor Garden at Grandchester Manor, police suspicion falls upon his son Robert. In desperation, Sir Richard turns to his friends Felix Heron and his wife Thelma to help clear his son's name. To the initial annoyance of the police, the private investigator and his wife join the house guests and set to work to solve the mystery. But when two more murders rapidly follow, it looks like the detective duo may finally have met their match . . .